FIREWATER

Nick Carson, a lone traveller, Pierre Gamont, an unscrupulous half breed, and Slick Hartnell, a ruthless outlaw, all sought an untold fortune in gold. The problem was that it lay in Indian territory. The Indians, under the leadership of Glorious Smile, a white woman captured as a baby, were gradually absorbing western civilization and were well aware of the harmful effects of alcohol. Consequently, when Gamont sold whiskey to a renegade Indian in return for gold, the tribe took to the warpath . . .

Awarded for excellence
to Arts & Libraries

Kent
County
Council

JED McCLOUD

◆

FIREWATER

Complete and Unabridged

LINFORD
Leicester

First hardcover edition published in
Great Britain in 2000 by
Robert Hale Limited, London

Originally published in paperback as
'Firewater' by John Russell Fearn

First Linford Edition
published 2003
by arrangement with
Robert Hale Limited, London

British Library CIP Data

McCloud, Jed, *1908 – 1960*
    Firewater.—Large print ed.—
Linford western library
1. Western stories
2. Large type books
I. Title II. Fearn, John Russell, *1908 – 1960*
823.9'14 [F]

ISBN 1–8439–5057–X

Published by
F. A. Thorpe (Publishing)
Anstey, Leicestershire

Set by Words & Graphics Ltd.
Anstey, Leicestershire
Printed and bound in Great Britain by
T. J. International Ltd., Padstow, Cornwall

This book is printed on acid-free paper

1

The creak of wooden wheels, the flapping of torn canvas in the hot wind, the snorting of game but weary horses, the shouts of men — as the caterpillar of the settlers' wagons wound its way steadily through the blazing sun of southern Kansas.

It was mid-afternoon in the late spring of the year. Grant Hansford, leader of the settlers, sat on the hard driving seat of his wagon, accustomed to its eternal jolting, and looked out across the wastes. The view was little different from that which he had seen all the way from northern Ohio, where the caravan trail had started.

Desert, sunlight, distant hills, water-holes, and rivers few and far between. California and its gold was the eventual destination, but before that goal could be reached there loomed one very real

1

danger . . . Redskins.

Grant Hansford was thirty, tough as whipcord, his lean face nut-brown with exposure, his eyes of the fearless blue found in the pioneers and explorers. He chewed a worn pipe as he looked about him, his sinewy hands holding the reins of the sweating team. Back of him, under the canvas, his wife and baby daughter lay cushioned between bed-rolls to absorb the shocks and bumps of the rutted ground, the worn canvas protecting them from the murderous blaze of the sun.

'Hey, Grant, d'yuh reckon it's safe ter keep goin' or do we camp fur the night?'

Grant peered round the angle of the canvas as a bearded giant astride his sorrel came speeding up. His was the unenviable job of keeping the wagons more or less in formation as they rumbled onwards.

'Gettin' a bit ahead of yuhself, Mike, ain't yuh?' Grant asked, grinning. 'It's only mid-afternoon yet and yore talkin'

2

about goin' to sleep.'

'I said camp!' the big fellow retorted. 'We're nearly outa Kansas now. Before long we'll cross the north-west tip of Oklahoma, then we'll be in New Mexico. Once that happens we're in Indian country, and just anythin' can happen, I reckon. We don't wanter be worn out if there's trouble.'

'Yeah,' Grant agreed thoughtfully, his eyes slitted towards the shimmering distances. 'Mebbe yore right. The thought of them Pueblos in New Mexico and Arizona, both of which territories we've gotta cross, have bin givin' me plenty to worry over. Jus' the same, it's too early to camp right now. I figger we oughta push on 'til evenin'. By that time we should ha' reached Des Moines, an' that's as good a place as any.'

'Have it yuh own way,' the giant responded, and swung his sorrel away to continue his job as formation-leader.

Grant Hansford did have his way; he saw to it that he always did. There was

3

no other way to control the men, women and children who were in his care and under his authority. So the procession continued on its way through the grilling afternoon. Save for a halt at Cimarron River, Grant Hansford permitted no let-up. By early evening the tip of Oklahoma was being traversed — and at sundown Des Moines, rugged territory near the foot of Fisher's Peak, was gained.

The wagon wheels ceased turning. The horses relaxed. Men, dusty and sweating, leapt down from their hard wooden seats to get their orders from the leader. The womenfolk began to appear, moving with silent efficiency, accustomed by now to the demands made on them for food when camp was pitched.

In the space of an hour the wagons had been drawn up in a wide circle around the camp, chiefly as a safeguard against possible attack. In the immediate centre of the camp, sprawled on the rocky earth, the men and women took their meal under the stars, their faces redly lighted by the crackling fire. Here and there a very young child cried. The older children romped but did not stray beyond the immediate circle of wagons. Nearby, tightly corralled, the horses nodded sleepily now that they had been fed and watered.

'Everything okay?' Grant Hansford asked his wife, as she sat beside him eating her meal.

'Couldn't be anything else with you, Grant.' Her slim hand gripped his for a moment and he gave a smile. Ruth, with her golden hair and frank blue eyes, meant all in the world to him. She was loyal, had courage, and yet remained a woman. No man could ask for more.

'She seems to have stood the journey okay so far,' Grant commented, glancing down at the two-year-old who was sleeping contentedly between them.

'Betty?' Ruth gave a smile as she studied the mop of golden curls and innocent face in the starlight. 'She'll stand anything, Grant. She's a pioneer, like her mom and dad.'

Grant nodded and was silent for a moment. He lighted his pipe, surveyed the talking men and women around him, then fell to deep thought. It was Ruth who presently interrupted him.

'Anything wrong, Grant? I've seen you looking worried once or twice on the journey.'

'Just weighin' things up,' he shrugged. 'Ain't so easy to be the leader of this mob of people. A lot uv responsibility attaches, I reckon.'

'You don't fear that we'll never reach California, do you?'

'We'll reach it, Ruth — or rot in the desert. That's what we came fur. For gold — a new life — a new start. We knew that when we set off. All uv us did.'

'It's the thought of Indians that bothers you, then?'

'Partly. I guess we might have a brush with 'em anywheres in this region, or Arizona. The Pueblos are mighty plentiful hereabouts, nearly as thick as the Algonquians and Iroquois in the Ohio Valley and Mississippi Basin. But it ain't exactly that which bothers me. We can deal with 'em with rifles. It's Slick Hartnell who has me worried.'

Ruth said nothing. Her gaze wandered into the circle of chatting men and women. At a fair distance she spotted Slick Hartnell smoking a black cheroot and surveying the stars idly. Young, oily, a dude in his dress despite the rigours of the trip, he had already shown that he considered himself irresistible to women — and Ruth in particular.

'I trust you to th' end uv the earth, Ruth,' Grant murmured, 'but every time I come near that guy Hartnell I feel like putting a slug in his belly. I don't like him. He's already caused a heap uv trouble among the married folk. Mebbe he oughta be left hog-tied somewheres on the trail.'

'You can't do that, Grant — and you won't. Slick's as entitled as anybody to get to California. He joined us in Illinois and he's done his share of the work since. Besides, he's handy with his gun on occasions.'

'He should keep his place,' Grant snapped — and then, as though he had caught the thoughts of the two discussing him, Slick got to his feet and came ambling over, hands in pockets, six-gun slapping against his powerful thigh.

'When do you reckon we'll hit California, Hansford?' he asked, pausing a few feet away with his thumbs latched in his pants belt.

'Soon as we can. I ain't sayin' no more'n that.'

Slick grinned, white teeth gleaming in his handsome face.

'What's the matter, fella?' he asked. 'Can't I ask a simple question without you gettin' sore?'

Grant made to get up quickly, but the restraining arm of Ruth stopped him. Slick considered the pair of them, then his eyes strayed to the sleeping child.

Finally he looked at Grant again.

'You ever stop to think, Hansford, what'll happen if the Redskins see this wife of yourn? She's white, hundred per cent pretty, and worth any Indian's attention. They might take her and — '

'Shut up!' Grant broke in savagely, and, whipping free of his wife's grip, he got on his feet. Slick did not move, but his right hand lowered from his belt to his revolver butt.

'Okay, only warning you.' Slick spoke lightly, a definite education in his voice. 'I think this trek to California is crazy anyways, but I'm in on it 'cos I like gold as much as the next man, and I can't get to it without company. Too dangerous with Pueblos around. But it isn't the place for women as pretty as Ruth.'

'I never gave yuh permission to call her 'Ruth',' Grant said grimly.

'Guess you didn't; neither did she. But we're all friends in this outfit, surely?'

'Look, fella — ' Grant's hand shot

out and gripped the front of Slick's shirt. 'Yuh'll keep your distance from here on, see? I know yuh've been a durned nuisance 'cos she's told me as much — an' yuh haven't exactly ignored the rest of the good-looking women in our bunch either. Keep on doin' it an' yuh'll find yuhself ditched somewheres on the trail with only the buzzards to know what happened to yuh. Savvy?'

Slick hesitated over saying something — then instead he twirled round as an object flicked within a foot of him and landed with a thud in the side of the nearby wagon. He stared at the object blankly — An arrow, still quivering.

'Indians!' Grant gasped. 'We're being attacked — '

He was right. The first arrows were followed by a volley, and beyond the wagons came the whooping of the attackers in the darkness. The assembled men and women scrambled to their feet and raced for their rifles. Grant bawled his orders at them, put his still-sleeping daughter in the wagon and then lay down beside Ruth with the wagon wheels for protection. He levelled his six-gun, proud of the fact that Ruth, able to handle a rifle well, was at his side.

For a time the arrows flew thick and fast, and here and there a man or woman fell — but the blaze of guns was evidently more than the Redskins could stand, for after a while the onslaught ceased and the night was quiet again.

Grant began moving again at length. Ruth gave him a nod to assure him she was okay, so he moved back to the centre of the encampment to assess the casualties. Three men and a woman had been lost, all of them dead from direct arrow hits. A remaining one was badly wounded and in the care of the one not-very-efficient doctor in the outfit. His announcement that the arrows were poisoned did not help very much either.

With grim eyes, Grant looked about him. The dead must be buried and the one wounded man taken care of. Then he glanced to his left as Slick Hartnell came lounging up, holstering his six-gun as he did so.

'They'll be coming back,' he said, his leanly-handsome face gleaming with perspiration. 'We've a fight on our hands, Hansford.'

'Yuh don't haveta tell me,' Grant snapped.

Slick eyed him for a moment. 'I think you got me figgered wrong, Hansford. I can do more things than look at a pretty face. I got four of those blasted Indians with my hardware.'

'So what? When it's your life or theirs you ain't likely to pull your punches, Slick. What's the idea? Tryin' to win favours frum me or somethin'? If so, yore wastin' your time.'

'I was just thinking. You're the leader of this bunch — but if something happens to you, as it well might with these feathered beauties on our hands, what happens? At a time like this you oughta delegate.'

'And name you deputy, I s'pose?'

Grant asked coldly.

'No reason why not. I know how to shoot better'n any guy around here — 'cept you — and somebody's got to take control if anything goes wrong.'

'I can look after myself,' Grant retorted. 'Stick to yuh own side of the fence, Slick, and don't bother me.'

Grant turned away angrily and set about the task of arranging for the burial of the dead. It was accomplished without interruption, the last rites performed. Then Grant looked on the men and women around him.

'Prepare for more trouble,' he warned. 'Harness the horses to the wagons in case we have to dash for it. Have all ammunition to hand.' He glanced up at the moon breaking through ragged cloud. 'I guess that isn't going to help us,' he added. 'Once these Redskins can see what they're doin' they'll double their attack. But so can we. Trust in Providence an' shoot straight. That's all I can say.'

He turned to go, then a man called

out: 'Say, boss, what happens if you're wiped out? Who's delegatin' fur you?'

'Nobody,' Grant snapped, looking about him.

'That ain't reg'lar,' a woman objected. 'We've gotta have a man to call on if you get rubbed out.'

'I offered to take on,' Slick remarked from the shadows. 'I guess Mr Hansford doesn't approve.'

'This ain't no time fur likes an' dislikes,' a nearby man said. 'None uv us has much time fur you, Slick, but yore a mighty fast shooter an' yore not worried by sentiment. I guess yuh'd do well enough if anything happens to th' boss.'

'Yeah — sure thing.'

Grant looked about him, his face grim. He could see Slick was grinning a little in the moonlight.

'Looks like you're outvoted, Hansford,' he commented drily.

Grant neither confirmed nor denied the decision. Without a word he returned to where Ruth was sitting with her back to the wagon-wheel, a rifle across her knees.

'You should give the people a lead, Grant,' she murmured. 'They expect it. Personalities don't enter into it and I think Slick's the best man to follow you.'

'Everybody around here seems mighty sure I'm goin' t'die,' Grant snapped. 'You included. Or mebbe that guy means something t'yuh?'

'You know better than that, Grant.'

'Yeah — guess I do.' He looked shamefaced in the moonlight. 'I shouldn't have said that, Ruth. I'm sort of edgy.'

Ruth said no more, prepared to accept Grant's explanation. She got up presently and crept into the wagon to be sure that Betty was still sleeping. She was, a line of moonlight crossing her passive face as she lay breathing deeply — then into the quietness there came the onslaught of the second attack.

Ruth turned sharply as an arrow went clean through the canvas and plunked into the woodwork near her.

Guns exploded. Betty awoke, screaming, to find herself enveloped in her mother's arms. Grant's head peeped in under the canvas.

'Keep down.' he ordered. 'Lie flat, the both of yuh, else yuh might stop an arrow. This looks like the real thing — '

It sounded like it too. As she flung herself on her face, protecting the whimpering child, Ruth was aware of the yells of the invading hordes, the thwack of arrows, and the explosion of guns from around her. For a time Grant remained in the protection of the wagon wheels, sniping as best he could at the moonlit figures flitting by, some on foot, others on horses — then he swung in alarm as incendiary arrows began to arrive, landing in the more distant wagons and setting canvas and woodwork aflame. Those womenfolk who were guarding their children came blundering out into the smoke, clutching their precious burdens, sometimes dropping in their tracks as an arrow struck them.

Grant jumped up and sped swiftly to the nearer wagons, tearing out the flaming arrows savagely and stamping on them. He sniped as an Indian flew past and brought him crashing. Then Slick came running up, guns in his hands.

'No use fightin' this lot, Hansford,' he snapped. 'You'd better give the order to get goin' — the lot of us. These murdering devils'll have our scalps before we know it.'

'I'm giving the orders here,' Grant retorted. 'Shut up and get busy with your hardware.'

Slick breathed hard; then his hatred for Grant suddenly spilling over he slammed out his right-hand gun, butt foremost. Grant folded up, stunned, his gun dropping. Slick twirled round and surveyed the confusion for a moment, then he darted across to Grant's caravan and hauled himself up under the canvas. Ruth turned a worried face in the moonlight.

'Bad news, Ruth,' Slick said briefly.

17

'Grant's stopped an arrow. I'm making a dash for it if I can. You use your rifle from the back of the wagon whilst I drive.'

'What about the rest of the folks?' Ruth cried, too distraught to fully grasp what Slick had said.

'They must look to themselves. My job's to protect you an' the kid. Grant would have wanted that — '

Slick settled on the driving seat and lashed the whip over the withers of the frightened horses. They jolted, already half panic-stricken by the whirring of the arrows and crash of gunfire. On this Slick was relying. He knew they'd travel like hell — and he was also pretty sure that in the confusion he might make a getaway without the Redskins noticing.

After that — Well, with Ruth to himself there was a good deal he meant doing. When he took a fancy to a woman he went to any length to get her. The baby did not signify: he could ditch the kid somewhere once he got clear.

He drove like the devil, the wagon bouncing and rattling on the uneven ground, Betty crying piteously at the concussions which shook her. Ruth was too busy to pay attention. With the canvas slightly parted at the back of the wagon she was resting her rifle on the woodwork and sniping as carefully as she could at the three Indian braves who were pursuing in the moonlight.

She had no time to be frightened, no time to be grief-stricken at the death of her husband. Again and again her gun exploded — and presently one Indian fell from his horse. She sighted again, then paused at the alarming vision of a horde of Redskins riding up from the left. To take care of all of them was impossible.

'Slick!' she cried hoarsely, over the din of the wagon. 'We can't get out — ! We're stuck in an ambush or something — !'

Slick did not answer. He had already seen what was coming. He glanced quickly into the darkness of the wagon and could descry Ruth's figure; then he started as she suddenly shrieked and clapped a hand to her forehead, falling backwards and narrowly missing the screaming child.

Slick released the reins and stumbled into the wagon, lifting the fallen girl quickly. He lowered her again as the moonlight revealed an arrow embedded deep in her forehead, its shaft broken off as she had fallen. He listened for her heart, but it had ceased beating.

'Dog-gone,' he muttered, setting his mouth — then he looked up with a start at the thunder of approaching hooves. Stumbling over the dead girl and the screaming child he reached the driving seat again — then jumped ahead on to the back of the right-hand horse in the team.

Savagely he slashed with his knife, cutting the animal free of the harness. Released from the strain of the wagon it shot forward on flying hooves, Slick clinging frantically to its neck, as he had to ride bareback. Faster and faster yet, gradually drawing out of range of the swirling braves circling the wagon. One or two made a half-hearted effort to follow him, then it occurred to them there was plenty worth looting in the wagon and they returned to it, rejoining their fellows.

Two of them climbed over the rear of the wagon, tore away the canvas so as to provide light from the moon, and then began a search. Ruth's dead body was examined, then rolled to one side as the arrow through her brain was discovered. Provisions and ammunition were thrown overboard, together with spare rifles and pots and pans, all useful accessories to the Redskins.

Then one of the bare-chested braves raised the lustily bawling Betty in his hands and peered at her in the silvery light. He considered for a moment and then set her down again, drawing his keen hunting knife. Before he could plunge the blade into the weeping child his wrist was seized firmly and he found himself looking into the impassive face of his chief, White Cloud.

'White baby — we take,' he announced. 'Hair of gold. She different. Do not harm her.'

The brave returned his knife to its sheath and picked up the child obediently, jumping to his horse from the wagon with Betty clutched in his sinewy arms. She still cried, though with less vehemence. Tiredness was beginning to overtake her.

White Cloud descended to the ground also and stood watching until everything worthwhile had been transferred from the wagon to the backs of the horses, then he gave his impartial nod.

'Destroy,' he ordered, still using the tribal language, 'By fire.'

The command was obeyed. In a matter of minutes the wagon was blazing in lonely fury in the midst of the desert, the braves riding away from it, back to the scene of their onslaught a couple of miles distant. With them went Betty Hansford.

Behind, the wagon became the funeral pyre of Ruth, perhaps from a fate infinitely more terrible.

★ ★ ★

Grant Hansford stirred slowly, his fingers clutching ploughed-up dirt, his head throbbing with the hammers of Hades. In his nostrils was the stench of burning wood and flesh; in his ears the crackle of fire. But the sound of yelling Redskins and the crash of guns had ceased.

Slowly he struggled to his feet and felt the sticky blood at the back of his head. Then, his brain clearing, he remembered. Slick! The blow he had dealt — ! Grant looked about him in horror. Wagons were burning furiously on all sides, most of them filled with bodies already dead. About the centre of the clearing men and women lay prone. Presumably he had been mis-taken for dead and left untouched; those that lived had been taken away

— for worse than death.

He looked towards the spot where his wagon had been standing and then raced towards the empty space. He forgot everything else as he saw wagon trails leading out under the moonlight into the empty desert. He had only one concern — to find his wife and child. To find Slick also, whom he was convinced was at the back of their disappearance.

Regardless of possible attack from remaining Indians he went on doggedly, following the wagon trail. He was not attacked. The Redskins, their blood-lust satiated, had retired long since to their own hidden compound.

He came at last upon the still smoking embers of the wagon. Going on his knees and searching the debris with a stick, he found his worst fears justified. He came across the scorched remains of a bracelet Ruth had been wearing; a twisted brass plate which still carried his name upon it — and more horrible still, the bleached javelins of bones.

It was dawn before the stunned man realized what had happened. His wife and child burned to death in the wagon — If Slick was responsible he too had probably paid the penalty by now at the hands of the Redskins. If by some grotesque twist of Fate he had escaped, then . . . then he must be found.

Grant got on his feet shakily, his gaunt face still wet with tears. But for the treachery of Slick he, Grant, might have died beside his wife and child, perished as all pioneers expect to perish in the attainment of their goal. But to be struck down, and awaken to this — !

'If you still live, Slick Hartnell, God help you,' Grant whispered, clenching his fists. 'I'll find you — and kill you — even if I go to the ends of the Universe!'

He began walking, he knew not where. The dawn was coming in all its glory, but he heeded it not.

2

To 'Glorious Smile' the savage Pueblo tribe did not appear savage. The womenfolk of the tribe treated her kindly. Then into her slowly-maturing comprehension there came the men — warriors most of them, ruled by the aged but resolute White Cloud.

Glorious Smile, as she grew older, moving with the tribe on their various nomadic excursions, began to realize that she was something apart from them. They were red: she was white. They had black, lank hair and cruel eaglelike faces: she had golden hair, rudely cut with a knife to shoulder level, and the waters of the lakes told her her eyes were as blue as the sky.

She watched the onslaughts on white people like herself with a child's dispassionate interest. She neither approved nor disapproved of cruelty and the tribal rites. She had watched white men and women die and she had not flinched. She was neither heartless nor ruthless: she simply reflected the environment in which she was growing up . . . then one day she knew she was of a race apart.

In a half-looted caravan after a massacre she found books and maps, pencils, pictures, all manner of things. Glorious Smile began to learn.

At the age of twelve she had learned enough to talk halting English instead of the curious 'several-words-in-one-sentence' used by those among whom she lived. She knew she was in a world where civilizations existed; that she was on a continent not yet ruled by law and order, where every encroachment of the white man forced the Redskins further back from their hard-earned territories. In one way she hated the whites for driving her benefactors before them; in another she was curious to know the ways and habits of people with a skin like her own.

And she continued growing. White Cloud was proud of her. He had believed she had the makings of a goddess on the night he had ordered her to be unharmed; now, as he was growing into an old man and she into a young woman he was sure he had not been mistaken. Life in the open air had made of Glorious Smile a sleek-limbed young woman with a gaudy Indian sarong barely covering her perfect body.

The braves of the tribe who had grown up with her were increasingly fascinated by her white skin and perfect form, yet none of them dared to ask White Cloud that they might take her as a squaw, for she was not as they were.

At the age of twenty the girl realized her life with the tribe had evidently not been without purpose. As she lounged one day amidst the rocks, bathing in the furious heat of the sun, White Cloud came to her. He stood for a time watching her impartially, not a flicker of movement on his hatchet-face.

The girl caught sight of him at last and half rose. She was ready to make her usual obseisance before him, but he raised a hand imperiously and prevented her. Then he began speaking, using the broken English the girl had taught him.

'The hour has come, Glorious Smile, when White Cloud will hand over his power. White Cloud has watched you. He is well pleased.'

'With me?' the girl asked surprised. 'But, White Cloud, I have done naught but — '

'Enough! I have spoken, Glorious Smile. Before I make peace with my gods it is law that I name my successor to rule the tribe. It shall be as I have spoken; you shall rule.'

The girl's blue eyes looked at him in wonder. She rose slowly upright — tall, smooth-limbed, her skin golden brown. Moving forward, she caught at the chief's hand.

'White Cloud, do you really believe that the rest of the tribe will wish that? I am different — not of your race — '

'You are white,' the old man answered, his face impassive. 'The white race is highly intelligent; none but the veriest fool would deny it now. They are fearless. They attack. They drive us before them. I in my wisdom believe that you, who are also white, will fill my warriors with the fire of your race and lead them to recover much that they have lost. You have learned much. You have taught me much. I have spoken.'

'You believe, White Cloud, that you are going to die?'

'Before many moons I shall make peace with my gods. I shall be content, for you shall rule.'

The girl was silent. She knew the custom of the tribe: that the old should walk away to die after a ceremonial dedicated to the ancestors of the race — but she was not old enough to recall the initiation of a ruler of the tribe. She knew the responsibility it entailed. Her white instincts made her wonder just how the less loyal spirits would react.

To the Redskin the white was the bitterest enemy. Under White Cloud's protection she had lived happily, but now . . .

'Have no fear, child,' the chief said presently, as though he were reading her thoughts. 'You have the power and courage to bear yourself well. Tonight at the full of the moon I shall name you.'

With that he turned and walked away with his regal silence. Glorious Smile remained where she was, looking about her. The men and women of the tribe were not aware of what was coming. They were tilling the ground, picking crops, washing clothes in the distant river, attending to the horses. It was all very primitive, and, being a scale removed from the primitive, the girl began thinking.

She returned to her couch in the rocks, soaking in the blazing heat. She had always believed there was no need for the constant nomadic movement of the tribe. Civilizations had cities, so the books said — so why not the Pueblos?

31

For by this time she knew the name the whites had for her particular tribe. There were the Iroquois and the Algonquian tribes, too. Far away in the Mississippi Valley the Algonquians had built stone cities under the shelves of mighty cliffs and had domiciled themselves. So why not her own tribe?

The idea took possession of her. The Algonquians had central squares, terraces, places of government, even a well-developed social order, and out of this must of necessity spring a more rational and less savage aspect towards life. The cruelty of the tribe was something that now appalled her: the white woman in her wanted to stop it. Perhaps she might, as queen.

There was much she could do. Her imagination was aflame. The books said that to the south of the continent the highly-civilized Mayas were settling, but how long they would be able to survive under the onslaughts of the cruel Aztec Indians could not be told. The Aztecs seemed to be everywhere — inhuman, callous, masking their deadly natures under expressionless features. One could not fight tribes like the Aztecs and Iroquois without solid stone defences. So, as queen, her first move would be to have a city made.

She sat up and considered the position. The tribe was settled at the moment at the north-east corner of New Mexico, three miles or so from the River Moro and within the shadow of the Sierra Blanco mountains. The foothills of those mountains held countless natural cliffs, hollowed out beneath, in which cities of stone could be erected. It would mean protection from weather, defence against attack. With these joys to offer, Glorious Smile began to feel more certain of being able to justify her queenship.

She relaxed again, unaware of the tall figure higher up the rocks who was studying her. The figure turned away presently, came to ground level, then walked across the compound to where White Cloud had disappeared into his wigwam. The old chief, resting amidst his blankets with his squaw busy nearby, looked up in surprise as the young warrior entered.

Impassively, greetings were exchanged, then the young warrior spoke:

'Shining Fire overheard,' he said. 'White Cloud is making the paleface woman queen of the tribe. Shining Fire is not well pleased.'

White Cloud did not respond for a moment. Shining Fire was his own son — tall, powerful, stripped to the waist, his lank hair drawn into a knob at the back of his wellshaped head. The inherited cruelty of his race lay in the set of his mouth and chin. His dark eyes were smouldering but respectful.

'White Cloud is displeased,' the old chief said at length. 'Shining Fire failed in battle. You are no longer warrior, my son, but a coward.'

The young Redskin's features shifted for a moment and then became immobile again. His father spoke the truth. Somewhere in the make-up of

Shining Fire there was fear of something stronger than himself, but in the destruction of the weaker he was a warrior indeed.

'I have courage, my father,' he said presently. 'I have but to be tried in — '

'No, Shining Fire!' The old man shook his head adamantly. 'My choice is made. The tribe will not obey a coward. The white girl has courage, beauty and intelligence. You overheard my words with her. It is well you know my decision before the ceremony. I shall not change that decision.'

'My father, I — '

'I have spoken, Shining Fire.'

The young Indian set his rat-trap mouth and left the wigwam. In moody silence he wandered back to his rocky eyrie and settled down with the immovability of his race, watching the lithe girl who was sprawled in the sunlight further down the slope. He had always hated her. She had been brought up beside him, a foster-sister, and had always beaten him by superior intelligence.

Now she was to cheat him of the greatest prize of all — leadership of the tribe. Shining Fire's hand stole to the hunting knife in the leather thong about his waist, and he drew forth the keen blade. For a moment he held it in finger and thumb, his piercing eyes sighted on the reclining figure some distance below him. In that moment he had the power of life and death in his hand. With one flick he could unerringly fling the blade deep into the girl's left breast, barely concealed by the sarong she wore.

Then he hesitated. No — White Cloud would know the culprit and his wrath would be terrifying. There would follow the ordeal by fire and lingering death. Shining Fire, afraid of pain, gave a shudder.

He returned the knife to his thong and sat down again. There would be other ways later — when White Cloud was asleep with his ancestors.

★ ★ ★

It was early evening when the ancient buckboard and team came rattling into the tumbledown assortment of huts and buildings which called itself Medicine Lodge, on the Oklahoma-Kansas border. On the driving seat a swarthy, sun-blistered man in a battered sombrero and dust smothered pants and check shirt looked about him. His black hair and oily red skin would have stamped him as an Indian, a possibility lent added emphasis by his high cheekbones and steel-trap mouth. But in actual fact Pierre Gamont was a half-breed French-Aztec, making an indifferent living as a fur and general trader, supplying tribes and towns alike with his mysteriously-obtained wares. He used his French side when bargaining in the towns and became an Aztec when Indians had to be dealt with. In a sense he was a neutral, friend or foe of white or Indian as the mood pleased him.

At the moment his chief interest was in getting a drink. He had come a long journey and his throat was on fire. He kept on driving the weary team until he came to the Silver Dollar Saloon in the main street, then, with a thankful sigh, he jumped down from his wagonful of junk and knotted the horses' reins to the tie-rack. Later he would attend to the animals. For the moment his own craving must be satisfied.

The Silver Dollar was not very busy at this hour of the evening. That would come after sundown when there was nothing else for the inhabitants of Medicine Lodge to do but drink and make merry.

Pierre Gamont reached the bar-counter and ordered whiskey. He gulped it down, repeated the order twice more, then planked his money down and looked about him. Now that his thirst was slaked for a moment his next interest was in possible customers. Medicine Lodge was no new stopping place for him: he had been here before and done fair business, particularly with Clay Benton, the owner of the saloon.

At the moment Benton was not on view. There were only a few punchers, prospectors, and one or two women intended to liven the place up as the evening advanced.

'Clay around?' Gamont asked the bar-keep, and the bar-keep gave a shrug.

'Be in his office, I guess — No, there he is,' he broke off, and nodded to the big figure in a black suit just approaching the bar.

Gamont nodded and waited. Clay Benton was big, swarthy, and tough as they come. There was a look in his dark eyes, too, which Gamont did not particularly like.

'So you blew into town again, huh?' Benton asked, reaching the bar and pouring himself a drink. 'Got your gall, ain't yuh?'

'Who? Me?' Gamont looked innocent. He had the inherited gift of being expressionless when necessary. 'What did I do, anyway?'

Benton downed his drink and his

eyes narrowed. He had never liked Gamont particularly, even though he had done business with him. He just couldn't understand the man. He was handsome in a cruel kind of way, and some remote sort of education in his younger days had given him the gift of the gab. Trader though he might be, Pierre Gamont was no ill-spoken ruffian.

'I'll tell yuh what you did,' Benton said, answering the question. 'You sold me some furs last time you was here. They'd got a disease uv some sort. I put them on some of my gals for a show an' the durned things fell apart when they danced.'

'Was that so bad?' Gamont asked with a grin.

'Course it wus bad!' Benton blazed at him. 'Them gals of mine were nearly dancin' around with nothin' on 'em. It nearly started a riot. In stoppin' it I lost gallons of whiskey, hundreds of tumblers, three mirrors, and one of the batwings wus ripped off. I guess I oughta charge you with it.'

'Charge nothing,' Gamont responded. 'I didn't know the furs were wrong: just one of those things. As for charging me I guess you oughta pay me for accidentally puttin' on a leg show really worth having. Those gals of yours always did wear too much anyway.'

Benton considered, then his angry expression changed into a grin.

'Yeah — it certainly had something at that,' he agreed, reflecting. 'Okay, forget it. The whiskey you sold me was okay, so I suppose that balances things out.'

'Sure it does — and I've plenty more whiskey on the wagon if you want it. I make a point of not drinking my own stuff.'

'Not right now. You're two weeks sooner than usual coming round an' I'm not ready for buyin'. Try me next time.'

'Must be something that you're needing,' Gamont persisted, thinking of the burning miles he had covered. 'I guess it won't be furs after what happened last time, but I've harnesses, knives, a good line in guns — an' plenty of whiskey-tots to take the place of those you say got broken.'

'I got more frum the general stores,' Benton replied. 'I'll have 'em for nothin' — an' no other way.'

Gamont shook his head. 'That's not business, Benton, and I'm not interested. Okay, if there's nothin' I can do here this time I'll look in at the livery stables and general store and then bed down for the night. I've my cayuses to feed an' water yet, too.'

'Just a minnit, Gamont — don't be in such a hurry.'

Gamont hesitated, somewhat surprised, then turned back to the bar-counter. He took the whiskey Benton had ordered for him.

'I've a business proposition t' put to yuh,' Benton explained after a moment. 'S'posin' I could put you on to a source of plenty of gold and jewellery, how's about you an' me going fifty-fifty?'

'Gold and jewellery?' Gamont reflected

for a moment. 'If yore talkin' about trinkets, I'm not interested. No money in 'em.'

'I'm talking about all the gold you can carry, fella. The jewellery mightn't amount to much, but it's worth havin'. I guess.'

'Found a mine, or somethin'?'

'Nope — but I hear travellers' tales.' Benton wiped the back of his mouth with his big hand. 'I know a spot where there's gold for the pickin' up — and jewellery as well, mebbe, most of the stones bein' from settlers who've been attacked by Indians. The stuff's in an Indian settlement, but there ain't nobody who can get at it 'less he's got a special talent fur it. I reckon you could do it, Gamont. Yuh make friends of the Redskins when yuh want.'

Gamont looked puzzled. 'I guess the bit of gold taken from the settlers wouldn't be worth trying to get.'

'I said the *stones* had bin taken frum the settlers. The gold comes frum the gold-bearing veins where these Red-skins are livin'. The jiggers are sat right on top uv the stuff an' it don't mean a thing to them. You an' me could make use uv the stuff mighty quick if we could git hold uv it.'

'Give me another whiskey,' Gamont said, and drank it whilst he thought further. Then he said, 'What's all this about travellers' tales? If nobody can get near the gold, how come you know all about it?'

'I got the information first from a guy who fell foul of the Indians but managed to escape. I didn't believe what he told me so I went for a look-see myself an' risked my life doing it. What I saw convinces me there's gold fur the picking up. There must be when the walls of the buildings in some cases are made of gold-bearing rock!'

'Huh?' Gamont ejaculated, startled.

'I thought that'd shake you,' Benton grinned. 'An' it's a fact — but just how much gold there is lyin' around it isn't possible to find out without gettin' right inter the Indian town and takin' a look-see. That's what I want yuh to do 'cos yore the only man who can. Make any kind of deal yuh like, but bring back all the gold yuh can lay your hands on. Those Indian boneheads have no durned use fur it anyways.'

'Where is this town?' Gamont demanded. 'I never heard of any round here. I know the Algonquians have built towns of their own in the Mississippi Valley, but I never heard of any around here.'

'I'm not tellin' yuh the spot until we've made our deal, Gamont. An' I'll tell yuh something else — It ain't a matter of just dealin' with Indians and their chief. There's a white girl ruling 'em. I know it's a queer set-up, but it's the truth. I guess she's becomin' somethin' of a legend among travellers around here. Frum what I hear, she rules the whole Indian set-up, and probably she's back uv the Indian town being built. I guess a white girl with brains would be a durned sight more intelligent than the smartest Algonquian

45

Indian . . . In this region yuh'll be dealing with Pueblos. They might listen more ter reason than any other breed.'

'I think yuh handin' me a yarn,' Gamont said finally. 'A white woman rulin' an Indian tribe? It's crazy!'

'Plenty of more civilized Indians have married white women, Gamont, so I don't see that it's so loco workin' the other way around. I'm just warning yuh, that's all. Yuh may make a deal with the Indians 'cos yuh know how to handle 'em — but this white dame is of a different order.'

'For gold I'll risk all the white women in existence,' Gamont grinned. 'Mebbe even marry her if I haveta. Where is this place?'

'Is our deal of fifty-fifty on the gold agreed to?' Benton asked.

'Yeah — sure thing.'

'Naturally, I don't trust you,' Benton said frankly. 'I guess I wouldn't trust a half-breed any further than I could kick him, an' you ain't any excepshun. So I'll tell yuh what I'm doing — There are only four ways outa that Indian town an' I'm going to have every one of 'em covered with my boys. If you get into the town and out uv it in one piece, they'll pick yuh up and give yuh an escort back here: then yuh can tell me how far yuh've got. I'm not trustin' yuh with gold without knowin' what yore doin' with it. If by some chance yuh try to escape with some yuh'll not get far. Your trail'll be followed and yuh'll be shot down. Savvy?'

Gamont shrugged. 'Have it your own way. I've no reason for wantin' to gyp you, Benton — not with the number of gun-hawks you have on your side — Now, where is this place?'

'North-east corner of New Mexico — 'bout three hundred miles from here. The town's under a natural ledge in the Sierra Blanco Range, 'bout three miles frum the River Moro. Yah'll have plenty uv hillside trees fur cover.'

'Three hundred miles, huh?' Gamont made a face. 'It'd better be worth it when I get there.'

'Yuh get an escort there,' Benton said. 'Start tomorrow at daybreak and I'll have half-a-dozen men ridin' with yuh. Not only fur your own protection against possible trouble — but ter keep an eye on yuh, too.'

Gamont grinned. 'Seems like you've forgotten I roam around the territory by myself, Benton — but if that's the way you want it, okay. Daybreak it is. I'll spend the night at Ma Lawson's.'

Benton nodded and the half-breed turned away and left the saloon. When he had reached his wagon and team he stood thinking for a moment; then he climbed up to the driving seat and drove the horses to the livery stable further down the street. Here he spent some fifteen minutes watering and feeding the animals, but afterwards, instead of heading back again for Ma Lawson's rooming-house, he drove out of town by the southern trail and kept on going for an hour — then he turned the team aside into a deep gully and drew to a halt.

'Guess that critter Benton's got some queer ideas about my safety.' he murmured as he unharnessed the horses from the shafts. 'We rest here for two or three hours, mebbe, and then get going again. By the time it's daybreak we'll be a good fifty to eighty miles ahead of those owlhooters of Benton's.'

He led the two horses to the shelter of an overhanging rock, made sure they were hobbled, and then returned to the wagon and lay down amidst the junk, pulling a fur over himself. He slept soundly under the stars and awoke again whilst it was still dark. He judged from the sky that he had been asleep for three hours or so, which still gave him plenty of chance to get a move on.

He had a very early breakfast, fed and watered the horses again, then got them back between the wagon shafts.

By the time the dawn was approaching his buckboard was trundling along on the border of Kansas with only a few miles to go to the north-western tip of Oklahoma.

He knew his way with complete intimacy. In the course of years of selling his wares he had been in and out of almost every State. He grinned to himself as he drove along in the rising sunlight. Way back in Medicine Lodge Benton and his boys would probably be quite peeved to find their ambassador to the Indians had vanished, but the leeway they had to make up was considerable and Gamont was reasonably sure he could hit the Indian town before them.

He paused ever and again at water-holes and rested the sweating horses. They were in reasonably good shape since he had not flogged them into any excess of energy. Nevertheless, three hundred miles in the rising, grilling heat was too much to ask of any pair of animals, so when he reached Camp Nicholls on the Oklahoma border Gamont changed his animals and set off again with two well-rested vigorous sorrels in the shafts.

By noon he had left Oklahoma and

entered the north-eastern tip of New Mexico. He stopped for a while, then drove on again — grimy, sweating, wearied with the everlasting bouncing of the wagon and the intense blaze of the summer sun. He would have camped for a good twelve hours had he not been haunted by the thought that somewhere behind him Benton's men were probably in pursuit — and if there was gold for the picking up he meant to have it in his own way and tip off his friends the Pueblos to take care of any of Benton's boys they happened to see.

By mid-afternoon he rode into Des Moines and spent a full hour resting. To reach the River Maro and the Indian town in the Sierra Blanco he had a good seventy miles yet to cover — over some of the roughest territory so far. Des Moines marked the end of the desert trail which stretched back over the wilderness he had crossed: ahead was the mountainous district which, in peaks and valleys and hairpin bends, made up this entire north-eastern corner of New Mexico.

He decided it would be better to wait until sundown before carrying on. For one thing he wanted to rest himself and the animals: for another the darkness would cover his movements if by any chance Benton's men caught up and also it would shield him when he made his attempt to enter the Indian town.

In Des Moines he had the chance to verify from the inhabitants that the Indian town did exist, and so apparently did the white woman who governed it. The stories were various concerning her, but all remarked upon her beauty and the authority with which she ruled, until Gamont began to think she would prove every bit as interesting as the gold he hoped to find.

So, when the sun dipped behind the distant mountains, his wagon rumbled on its way again, losing itself presently in the mists of the valleys, and at length moving on steadily in the starry darkness which had closed down.

Gamont was driving mainly by

instinct now, using his infallible bump of direction to guide him towards the River Maro. He had passed it twice in his wandering life and felt pretty sure he could find it again. He drove up stony acclivities, along rough roads which the Indians themselves had made, across arid stretches of desert, and then presently through the heart of wooded country where the starlight was shut out and here and there a mountain freshet came tumbling from the heights.

Then at last through the thinning trees he beheld the River Maro, silver in the dawning moonlight. He smiled to himself, the two sorrels plodding stolidly up a long decline in the foothills. He had crossed the river further back by using a natural bridge of rock across a wooded gorge. Somewhere around here then there ought to be the town be was seeking.

He drew to a halt, alighted, then led the horses into the semi-circular clearing at the side of the trail. Unfastening them he hobbled their forefeet and watered them. Then leaving them nibbling at the roots around them he returned to the trail and surveyed.

From this high position the entire mass of the mountainous district was spread out before him, uncertain and grey in the moonlight. To the east lay the River Maro; to the west a stretch of timber country. Immediately before him was the slope of the mountain side ending in a deep valley. Then his gaze switched abruptly to a point a little to his right, perhaps three miles away. There was something red and gleaming there. It was presently joined by a second bright spot, then a third.

It was a moment or two before he realized he was looking at three distant campfires — and probably large ones; or maybe sacrificial pyres lighted by the Indians? If so, he was looking at his goal.

He made up his mind immediately and began moving, hoping that the fires would remain in being to guide him. They did, though he lost sight of them now and again as timber blocked his view in the forested portions. But at last, by dint of climbing, walking, and then running, he found himself at a rimrock from which he could gaze down on a natural rocky basin.

Flat on his face, partly screened by bushes, he gazed on a scene he had witnessed many times before — a Redskin festivity of dancing and singing. The noise was hideous to his ears, and the dancing was fantastic, the gleaming bodies lighted by fire and moon performing all manner of incredible gyrations. Though he was part Indian by descent, Pierre Gamont had never been able to make sense of these tribal customs.

Then after a while his gaze strayed from the crazy skirmishing before the fires to a dim vision of terraces and stone buildings beyond. He could make out the vague outline of streets, squares, and crude stone façades, some of them gleaming in lined patterns where the light caught them. Gold?

Abruptly the dancing ceased; the queer music stopped. Gamont froze, wondering if he had been the cause of the cessation. If so, he was ready to explain himself — and knew he could get away with it: but apparently it was the woman who now came into the midst of the dancers who had called the halt. Gamont gazed down on her in amazement, the firelight catching her perfect figure and the majesty of her movements. She said a few words and then moved on, settling finally on a massive stone throne and clapping her hands sharply.

The dancing resumed and the night became hideous again with the cacophony of the music.

Gamont stirred at last. He had not come all this distance to watch a grotesque carnival: he had business to do. Getting to his feet he moved silently through the bushes and then gradually worked his way to the side of the basin furthest from the white woman. He waited his chance, then as a Redskin came and stood nearby to watch the proceedings Gamont slipped out of hiding.

'I Pierre Gamont,' he said quickly, as the Indian swung round with his knife ready. 'Much business. Friend of Indian.'

The Indian hesitated, hearing his own tongue spoken by a stranger.

'Much bargaining,' Gamont continued, coming nearer with one hand on his gun in readiness. 'I brought you firewater once; I can bring it again. Make exchange.'

'Laughing Wind not understand,' the Indian growled back, his knife still in his hands. 'You paleface.'

'Like queen,' Galmont pointed out quickly. 'You are young, Laughing Wind. It is many moons since I came last. The oldsters will remember me. I brought much firewater. You dance to my firewater. Great happiness. Wondrous dreams.'

'Laughing Wind remember,' the brave said finally, and put his knife back in its sheath. 'Many moons ago, when White Cloud did rule us. You brought firewater. We drank. We laughed. We were happy. But not White Cloud. Much anger from him.'

'He didn't like his braves drinking firewater?' Gamont asked, slipping back into normal conversation for a moment; then he came to the tribal tongue again. 'But White Cloud dead now. Paleface girl queen. I hear stories that say so.'

'Glorious Smile is queen,' the Indian growled. 'She, like White Cloud, punish those who drink the firewater.'

Gamont hesitated. Naturally the tribal rulers did not approve of intoxicants being taken by their braves; it did queer things to their wild, savage natures — but there was no other way to barter for gold than through the Indian stomach; so Gamont, ever a salesman, tried again.

'Laughing Wind like the firewater?' he questioned.

'Laughing Wind never drunk the firewater.'

'You have got no idea what you missed,' Gamont murmured, and from his hip pocket took a flat bottle containing a small quantity of whiskey. He pulled the cork with his teeth and handed the bottle over.

The brave sniffed at the spirit, his face immobile in the light of the distant fires and pale moonlight. Then he drank the whiskey at a gulp, gave one cough, and stood pondering. His face remained inscrutable, but his naked feet shifted involuntarily as his nerves tingled.

'Laughing Wind like,' he decided finally. 'Much more.'

'Laughing Wind and the other braves can have all they want in return for yellow metal,' Gamont said, as the brave threw the empty bottle away. 'That is why I come. To make barter. To trade firewater for yellow metal. Gold.'

'Huh,' the Indian acknowledged, and waited.

'I hear stories,' Gamont persisted.

59

'There is gold in this town of yours. Gold in the stone out of which your town has been built. I want gold. Yellow metal. Plenty of same. Savvy?'

'Glorious Smile kill Laughing Wind if he give you gold.'

'Then Laughing Wind get no fire-water.'

There was silence for a moment. In the distance the noise of the festivity continued. Then Gamont spoke again.

'You like firewater. So do other braves. There is gold and to spare. Glorious Smile need never know you have taken any away. In this basin is gold for the picking up. I cannot take without you help me. Firewater your reward.'

'Much firewater?' the Indian said hopefully.

'Much,' Gamont agreed solemnly. 'If you add pretty stones and baubles to the gold you get still more. This is good palaver, my friend. For every piece of gold this size' — Gamont picked up a stone and handed it over — 'there will be firewater for a dozen braves.'

'Laughing Wind like,' the Indian decided at last, then looked surprised as he gave a hiccup. 'When you bring firewater?'

'Tonight. When the dancing ceases.'

'It is well. The dance ceases at the set of the moon.'

'Around four in the morning,' Gamont mused. 'Okay, I shall be here at the set of the moon,' he added to the Indian. 'This spot. You bring gold here. Tell nobody but the braves. If the queen finds out you die.'

The Indian nodded and, satisfied, Gamont melted into the darkness of the rocks and returned by the widest trail he could find to the spot where he had left his wagon and team. Apart from having arranged his deal, which he felt sure would be successful — knowing the fascination whiskey had for the Redskins — he had also found a rough track whereby he could drive his wagon to the edge of the basin.

Smiling to himself he fixed up a meal

in the moonlight, ate it, then prepared to wait until the moon had passed the zenith and was on its way behind the mountain range.

3

Pierre Gamont was not the only man who had seen the fires of the Redskins' tribal dance. Several miles to the south of where he had stopped, Nick Carson had also stopped. Negotiating treacherous mountain passes at night, and in Redskin territory, was no picnic for a lone man. He and his horse might plunge over the trail to instant death. By day, of course, there would be danger from the Redskins themselves, but Nick was satisfied that it was preferable to guard himself with six-shooters than fall headlong into a canyon by night.

Nick was twenty-five, and prospecting — otherwise he wouldn't have been in this sun-blistered glory hole in north-east New Mexico. Wearying of being foreman to a prosperous spread in Colorado and seeing his boss get all the kudos he had struck out south. His eventual destination, like all settlers and prospectors, was California, but knowing New Mexico and Arizona were not to be sneered at when it came to gold deposits he had detoured considerably on his journey.

Right now he sat with his back to a cliff wall, his horse fed and watered and nodding sleepily beside him. Nearby on the ground was the bedroll and camping tackle.

'Guess those Redskins must be loco, Blackie.' Nick spoke to his horse absently; his only listener. 'If they're not killing whites they're dancing their darned feet off. An' you and me had better vamoose quick from this region once daylight comes. I don't fancy fallin' in with a tribe of Pueblos. Though I can talk their tongue I don't think they'd listen to me.'

The horse scraped a foot in the pebbly ground in acknowledgment and Nick reached up and patted the animal's nose. Then he relaxed again, half asleep from the wearying ride he had made during the sunlit hours. He found he must have dozed for when he awakened with a start his back was stiff from resting on the rock wall and the moon had dipped beyond the mountain range.

He yawned, stretched his arms, then sat listening to a sound he had never heard before. It was like coyotes gone stark, blazing mad, wailing and screaming on the soft wind from somewhere in the now dark valley below him. But by degrees he realized that it was not animals which were making the noise but human throats. They were cries from crazed men —

Nick stood up, frowning into the darkness. All signs of the tribal dance had vanished. There remained only the hideous wailing — and after a moment or two he detected something else. It was the unmistakable sound of wagon wheels bouncing on rocky ground and coming ever nearer — apparently along the fairly wide trail which reached round the mountain on either side of him.

Nick waited, a gun in his hand in case of trouble: then after a while a wagon and team appeared in the dim starlight, being driven at a fair speed, but none the less with care. The driver pulled up sharply as Nick shouted at him.

'Hey, fella, are you loco, drivin' along this ledge in the dark? You're liable to go in the canyon.'

Pierre Gamont, on the driving seat, gave a little sigh of relief. For the moment he had thought that perhaps Benton's boys had caught up with him.

'You'd best be on your way, stranger,' he said. 'More than a chance that those Pueblos down there will come along here before long. An' they're blazing mad with whiskey, the whole darned lot of 'em.'

'Whiskey?' Nick repeated blankly. 'Where in heck did they get that from?'

'Me . . . ' And with with a lash of the whip Gamont set his wagon moving again before an investigation by Nick could reveal the gold-bearing ore amidst the furs.

Nick, however, was more bewildered than curious. He watched the wagon continue on its way and then scratched the back of his head.

'Guess we might do worse'n follow that guy, Blackie,' he murmured to his horse. 'The way he's carryin' on he'll jump clean off the rail before he's finished — an' if Indians come chasin' him he'll need more than himself for protection.'

Meantime, Gamont was driving on steadily, catching his breath now and again as the wagon swung dangerously near the edge of the mountain trail; but at last he began to thrash the horses across safer ground as one of the four clefts which led out of the valley came into view against the stars.

The crack of a gun made Gamont whip his own six-shooter into his hand and look about him anxiously. He could not see anybody amidst the frowning ledges of rock — but he did hear a voice from nearby.

'Stop yuh wagon, Gamont, before I drop yuh.'

Gamont tugged on the reins and the panting horses slithered to a standstill, harness jingling. Gamont sat watching as a trio of men came up silently, the dim light reflecting from their guns.

'Looks like we caught up, huh?' asked the man who had first spoken.

'Benton's gun-hawks, eh?' Gamont demanded, then he gave a rather shaky laugh. 'I figured you'd be turning up before long.'

'Yuh figgered right, yuh dirty half-breed. There's other boys watching the three other ways outa this valley. Guess we'll have to join 'em — but yuh won't be coming, Gamont. Git down from that wagon.'

Gamont had to obey. He stood watching, covered by guns, as the leader of the men made an examination of the wagon. By the time he had finished his voice was excited.

'Looks like the jigger did it, fellas!' he cried. 'There's enough gold here ter start a small mine.'

'That's what I went for, wasn't it?' Gamont snapped. 'Let's start off back for Medicine Lodge before those damned Redskins catch up on us.'

'I told yuh before, Gamont, you ain't goin' any place,' the leader snapped, jumping down again. 'You gave us the run-around an' that sorta changed Benton's plans. You figgered yuh could git the gold an' run out on him, didn't yuh? Yuh got it wrong. We're takin' the gold back to Benton and yuh'll get a bullet. The boss ain't got time fur double-crossers.'

The gun-hawk raised his six-shooter and sighted it, but before the hammer could drop and end things for the sweating Gamont there was a sudden explosion from the nearby rocks. The gun-hawk dropped his hardware, gasping with pain at the slug which had torn clean through his hand.

'Take it easy, you guys,' a voice

snapped. 'I'll blow hell out of the first one of you that moves. Throw your guns this way, towards my voice — an' hurry it up!'

The order was obeyed reluctantly by the remaining two men. The leader held his bleeding hand and said nothing. Then the dim figure of Nick Carson rode into view from behind the rocks, his guns at the ready in the moonlight.

'Three to one is too much in any language,' he snapped. 'Get moving, the lot of you!'

Grim-faced and muttering threats the gun-hawks turned towards their horses; then one of the trio ducked suddenly and whipped up a stone. The dim light prevented Nick from seeing exactly what was going on — but he knew fast enough when he was struck violently on the forehead. He half-slipped from the saddle, his guns lowering. Immediately the nearest gun-hawk dived for his hardware, but was brought up short as Gamont kicked him savagely in the face.

The second man, not taking the risk of trying to get his guns, made a dive at Nick instead and dragged him down to the ground, lashing up his fists at the same time. Nick staggered, still half-dazed from the blow of the stone, and his guns dropped out of his hands.

All the men bereft of weapons for the moment, they had nothing but their fists — and used them, all except the leader, whose damaged hand prevented him fighting. He began to sneak towards the nearest fallen gun.

With an effort, Nick brought his senses back into focus as he realized he was being hammered relentlessly. He jerked his head to one side and then slammed up a smashing blow to the jaw of his attacker. It found its mark and the man dropped, but in the interval the leader had picked up one of the guns and threw it with his left hand. Nick felt something batter his already-aching head and he crashed down in a blaze of whirling lights.

* ★ *

Upon the couch of furs within the stone building exclusively her own, Glorious Smile stirred uneasily, then awoke with a start. So rarely did anything disturb her sleep she could not imagine for a second or two what had brought her to the alert.

It was still intensely dark. No moonlight showed at the little oblong slit of window or under the fur stretched on a wooden frame across the entrance-way. Apparently it was that pitchy hour when the moon has set completely and the dawn was yet to come.

A sudden howling like the onslaught of animals brought Glorious Smile into a sitting position. The appalling noise increased into wild screams and shouts, amidst which was mixed a word or two of tribal tongue.

Glorious Smile scrambled from under the furs, whipped a gaudy blanket about her scanty night attire, and then took down a rifle from the wall. She only used it — a souvenir from a long-gone attack on a white party — when she felt her own safety was threatened. With it grasped in her hand, she flung aside the fur at the entrance and gazed out on to the starlit basin outside.

Not very far away the dim figures of dancing, yelling Indians were visible. They appeared to be taking flying leaps and then dashing inwards to a fixed spot and raining blows on something the girl could not see. She frowned and began advancing. It was not long before she came to a heap of wooden crates, some of them smashed in pieces, others still containing bottles. She whipped one out and peered at it, dimly able to descry the label.

'Whiskey!' she breathed, astounded.

That decided her. She had never seen the Redskins inflamed by liquor before, though she had been warned against it by White Cloud when he had made her queen. She flung the bottle away furiously and then hurried back to her dwelling.

Returning the rifle to its hook she took down a triple-thonged whip with a short butt. Gripping it firmly she strode outside again and across to where a dozen or so of the braves were flinging themselves in a mad orgy upon something on the ground.

'Hold!' she screamed at them, and the tails exploded over her head with the report of gunfire.

Her sudden arrival sobered the braves for a moment — then they made a rush towards her. Just what they intended doing she did not know. She swung the whip around in savage fury and the tails cut across the bare chests of the inflamed men as they came within a yard of her.

They fell back, swearing like dogs afraid of a tyrant. The girl held her ground even though her legs felt weak. So far she had never had crazed braves to deal with. If she failed now to exert her authority as queen her very life might be forfeit.

'You have drunk the firewater,' she yelled at them. 'I gave orders that firewater is not for braves . . . '

She broke off, suddenly realizing that the object on the floor of the basin was an Indian, face down, his back and shoulders brutally crushed by a succession of murderous blows. Obviously the Redskins had gone completely berserk. In their tribal customs they often bludgeoned an animal into extinction as a sacred rite, so the fact that they had selected one of their own kind and killed him in a similar manner was proof of their temporary insanity.

'You have killed a brother tribesman!' Glorious Smile shouted. 'For this the wrath of the rain gods will descend upon you! He will destroy our town and our people — You!' she broke off, and snapped the whip violently at the Redskin nearest her. 'Come here!'

He commenced to protest but the lash round his naked shins sobered him abruptly and he came forward.

'Whence came the firewater?' the girl demanded, and pointed to the crates nearby. 'Who gave you drink?'

'The paleface,' the young Indian answered sullenly.

'A white man came here, and gave you firewater?' The girl shook her head vehemently. 'I do not believe. Speak the truth, Grey Rain, before I command the ordeal by fire!'

The threat was sufficient. The Redskin went suddenly on his knees, his sinewy hands clawing at the blanket Glorious Smile had wrapped about herself.

'Grey Rain loves the firewater, Glorious Smile. So do other braves. We not know it was wrong.'

'You lie! I ordained it was wrong — many moons ago. Who was this paleface interloper? Answer me, Grey Rain!'

'He Indian — and paleface.' The brave grovelled in the dust at the girl's feet. 'Do much trading. He had palaver with Laughing Wind . . . '

As the Indian's face rose a little and his eyes glanced at the nearby dead body Glorious Smile went over to it, turned it on its back with the face to the stars.

'This is Laughing Wind,' she declared bitterly. 'You kill him, so he could not speak the truth to me! I still wait, Grey Rain, for the truth!'

'That is truth, Glorious Smile. The trader bargained with Laughing Wind. Firewater for yellow metal. Laughing Wind told me and my brothers. We helped him at the set of the moon.'

A glint in her eyes, Glorious Smile looked about her on the silent braves. Their madness seemed to have passed now. Fear of the lash and the dreaded ordeal by fire had sobered them.

'You mean a trader half-breed — white and Indian — sold you firewater in exchange for gold?' the girl asked, her voice quivering with fury.

'Paleface called Gamont,' Grey Rain got out quickly. 'Laughing Wind made the bargain and — '

'Silence!' the girl screamed at him, and brought her whip down across his bare shoulders. 'You shall suffer for this, Grey Rain! All of you will — ' She swung round and clapped her hands sharply together until at length a dozen or so braves began to appear, awakened from sleep, those of the tribe who had no deal in the whiskey for gold.

'Three of you imprison these brothers!' Glorious Smile commanded, pointing her whip to the delinquents. 'The rest of you scatter and find the paleface trader who brought firewater to this territory. Keep him alive. I seek to question him.'

Her orders were obeyed without question. The struggling and still half intoxicated Redskins were seized by their fellow tribesmen and bundled into the massive stone building which did service as a jail. The remainder, picking up more of their numbers on the way, faded into the dim starlight to trace Gamont's trail. To the Redskins, natural hunters, it was not a difficult task to follow the track Gamont had taken.

They pursued the trail up the valley side in swift silence, never speaking to each other, ready at any moment to deal death to anybody who interrupted their progress. As the dawn was approaching they gained the mountain path along which Gamont had driven his wagon. Here the trail was easy to follow.

At sun-up, the two dozen Redskins stealthily glided amongst the bushes surrounding a natural clearing at the side of the trail. Their keen eyes studied the scene. There was a wagon with two sleepy horses harnessed. Two men were lounging back against the rocks with guns ready for action. A third man was half lying down, his right hand wrapped in a blood-soddened kerchief. Nearby stood a solitary horse and beside it lay two men, tightly bound. The eyes of the watching Indians gleamed at the sight of the tied man on the left. It was Pierre Gamont, alive but obviously scared to death to judge from his expression.

One of the seated men opposite the

bound pair spoke.

'There's enough light now, Al, to git movin' and team up with the boys at the other passes. What are we waitin' fur? I'm gittin' kinda leary in this Indian country.'

Al nursed his bandaged hand for a moment before he replied. Then he looked at the sky.

'Guess yore right,' he assented. 'Weren't no use carryin' on in this mountainous region in the dark: only a guy as crazy as Gamont there would try it, anyways.'

'I still don't know why yuh don't shoot the jigger like you'd figgered on doin' at first,' another of the men growled. 'It's all extra trouble cartin' him an' that other guy around.'

'But worth it,' Al retorted viciously. 'I reckon a slug would ha' bin good enough fur Gamont to start with, but since on account uv him I got shot through the mitt I reckon he and that jigger who helped him oughta be ditched in the desert somewheres. Be slower an' more painful. Guys like that doesn't deserve a neat, quick getout . . . OK, let's move.'

Al got on his feet, quite unaware that a few yards away one of the Redskin braves had his sinewy right arm drawn back to the limit as he held his bow-string under tension. The arrow slammed home, dead true to its mark. Al gulped, looked stupidly at the shaft jutting from his left breast, then he folded up and dropped motionless.

Instantly his two comrades leapt up, firing their guns blindly at the surrounding bushes. Three of the Indians collapsed, hit more by luck than judgement, but the others fired unerringly. Al's henchmen dropped, one with an arrow through his neck, the other with his spine impaled.

Nick, fully conscious though firmly bound, lay watching anxiously as the Redskins appeared from behind the bushes and hurried forward, their knives ready, bows slung over their shoulders.

'I guess we can call it curtains, fella,' Gamont panted, his eyes wide with fright. 'These critters have caught the both uv us.'

Nick said nothing. He was steeling himself for an arrow or a knife, but to his surprise neither happened. Instead the Redskins cut down stout branches from the nearby trees, stripped them of leaves, then thrust them through the wrist and ankle cords of the two men. Supported thus, like cattle, Nick and Gamont found themselves being carried along the trail, the poles resting on the shoulders of the braves.

'I'd sooner they shot me an' ha' done with it than haveta go through what's comin' to us,' Gamont panted, rolling wild eyes in Nick's direction. 'When these critters get nasty even I can't talk 'em out uv it.'

'Mebbe you should have thought of that before you started sellin' firewater for gold,' Nick answered drily. 'Guess I should have my head examined too for trying to help you. I wouldn't have done only I don't like three pitching into one.'

Gamont had no more to say: he was too scared. He hung on his pole, watching anxiously as the valley side was traversed, and so at length the Indian town was reached. In the centre of the basin the poles were lowered, and the two men, their wrists and ankles grazed and bleeding, lay flat on their backs. Their faces impassive, the Indians retreated, taking their poles with them.

'I reckon this is the finish,' Gamont panted, looking around him on the distant stone buildings. 'The dame who runs this tribe won't show us much mercy, I guess.'

'Dame?' Nick gave a frown. 'What dame? You mean a squaw?'

'No — a white woman. Glorious Smile they call her — ' Gamont broke off and sucked in his breath. 'Say, will you look at those gold veins in the rocks there!' he whistled, his greed mastering his fear for a moment.

'No use looking, brother: it doesn't do us any good.'

Nick relaxed, straining uselessly at the cords holding his wrists. Then at the sound of approaching feet in the pebbly soil he screwed an eye round, and started. He saw a girl's shapely bronzed calves standing near him. His gaze went further, beyond her full thighs to the sarong — then up beyond her well developed breasts to her face. It was white, and stony, and beautiful, framed in a tumbled mass of golden hair caught back by a glittering ornament. In one hand she carried a triple-thonged whip.

'You Gamont?' she demanded, her blue eyes glinting.

Nick shook his head. 'No, lady. I'm just a harmless passer-by. This is Gamont . . . ' and he nodded to him as he lay cringing nearby. 'And I sure am surprised you're talking English — '

'You filthy carrion!' the girl spat. 'You have my gold stolen and my braves driven crazy by firewater . . . Where is the gold?'

'Back on the trail. You can have it, every rock of it, if yuh'll let me go.'

'Coward, too?' the girl sneered, and Nick, lying watching her couldn't help but notice the strength of her teeth. 'I might have known it. Only a coward would try and tempt a lot of savages just to get gold.'

'You speak mighty good English, ma'am for a Redskin-paleface,' Nick repeated. 'I figgered I'd have to talk in tribal tongue.'

'I'm a white woman,' she retorted, glaring at him. 'I can speak English as well as anybody. As for you, Gamont, you're going to be punished and the gold will be recovered.'

The girl turned and clapped her hands sharply. Sideways to the sunlight every curve of her lissom, powerpacked body lay revealed to Nick. He admired it in spite of the aura of danger. Gamont, however, was too scared to admire anything. The one dim hope he had was that, being a white woman, his punishment at her hands might not be so ruthless as that of a Redskin chief.

'Return to the trail,' the girl ordered to the braves who came running. 'Fetch yellow metal from this paleface's wagon. You others take him to the whipping post.'

Gamont half cried out and then stopped himself. The whipping post meant there would not be a sacrifice, so, with luck, he might yet escape with his life. He said nothing as he was picked up and hauled away across the stony expanse of basin floor.

The girl turned and settled beside Nick, one of her knees on the ground, the other bent. She considered him intently with her blue eyes just as though he were some peculiar animal.

'Outside the few settlers which my tribe have ambushed I have seen few men like you,' she commented.

'Yeah?' Nick gave a fleeting grin. 'If it's all the same to you, ma'am, I'd appreciate being allowed to go free. I've done nothing to your Indian braves and — '

'Then why do you go about with this jackal, Pierre Gamont?'

'I don't. I fell in with him when he was attacked. I tried to save him and got slugged — '

'I do not dis-discriminate,' the girl said, and she had a bit of a struggle with the word. 'You are a friend of Gamont's, therefore must be punished. I shall not kill. That is only for the very worst offences, such as attack on myself.' She stood up, erect as a goddess. 'I am the queen,' she explained.

'Uh-huh, so I gathered. And a durned pretty one. I hear they call you Glorious Smile. The smile isn't the only glorious thing about you.'

'Insulter!' she cried in fury, using a word of her own derivation. 'I not allow!'

Her whip cracked across Nick's broad chest, but not very fiercely; so he said no more. The girl turned and signalled to more of her braves. In consequence Nick found himself raised and carried across the basin floor. He was set down finally in a sitting position, his back to the jagged rocks, so that he faced both the whipping post and, nearby, a stone throne. Gamont was already secured to the post, his wrists crossed over the top of it, his feet secured at the base. He was sweating freely, his lank hair fallen down over his eyes.

Then came the girl herself, followed by the elders of the tribe. They took up positions on either side of her throne as she settled down and seemed to be thinking. Nick watched her, occasionally diverting his glance to his immediate surroundings. The nearest braves were some distance off, turned in respectful homage towards the girl. Which was just what Nick wanted. Placing him with his back to the rocks had been a good idea. He could feel their sharp edges against his pinned forearms. He began rubbing his wrist ropes fiercely over the jagged edge of the spur behind him.

The girl began speaking: 'Pierre

Gamont, you have stolen from this Indian town and bribed my warriors with firewater to do it. You have used your Indian ancestry to play a traitorous, thieving trick. Had you actually killed any of my braves death would have been your reward; since you did not, you shall be punished and then set free. I am a queen, but I am just. I shall decide with my advisers what your sentence shall be.'

She inclined her head towards the elders. Nick rubbed away furiously and felt a strand snap. Presently the girl rose and held up her white arm.

'You shall have fifty lashes, Pierre Gamont,' she announced. 'If their pain kills you that will not be my fault but your weakness. Let the sentence be carried out!'

She sat down again, her hands on the stone arms of the throne, her beautiful face implacable.

'She-devil!' Nick whispered, and with a final, savage strain of his powerful muscles he snapped the thong binding his hands. Just the same, he kept them together behind him, giving no clue that they were free.

Nick found himself wondering if the sentence upon Gamont had been her own idea or that of the elders. Probably she had to fall in with their suggestions even though she herself might not be in agreement. The fact remained that Gamont had not the physique to endure fifty lashes; he'd probably die around the thirtieth. And Nick had the added thought that he too might have to endure the same punishment.

He would have to act — and quickly. His hands were unbound. There must be some trick he could pull. Though he had no love for Gamont, he had less for the Redskins. Gamont was still above a Redskin in the scale of civilization.

Nick waited tensely until one of the braves, rippling with muscles, ripped the shirt from Gamont's back and then tested his whip with a vicious crack in the air. The girl and the elders remained silent, impassive, as motionless as the rocks —

Then Nick acted. He suddenly yelled blue murder and held his hands clasped behind him as he rolled and kicked on the ground. The girl glanced towards him and frowned; then, as he shrieked louder than ever, she stood up suddenly and raised her hand.

'Hold!' she commanded the brave with the whip, then, watched by every eye, she strode majestically across to where Nick was rolling violently. A foot or two away from him she stopped, gazing at him in wonder.

'Insects! Poison insects!' Nick screamed at her. 'Here, on the ground beneath me. See for yourself — ! They'll get all of you. I'm — I'm being bitten — to death — '

He screamed again and rolled. Still not understanding, the girl came forward and went on her knees to look at the ground. Nick watched her as he wriggled. She was between him and the nearest braves. She came closer and

Nick's hands suddenly came from behind him. One powerful arm encircled her waist, the other snatched her knife from the sash about her sarong.

'Let 'em shoot, if they dare!' he whispered as she fought savagely and uselessly to free herself. 'You're my screen, sweetheart — !' He slashed the blade through his ankle ropes and stood up, holding the girl in front of him.

The braves, their bows and knives ready, came forward slowly, but it was quite obvious to them that they could not possibly take aim at the white man without perhaps killing the girl, too.

'I'll have you killed for this,' the girl screamed, writhing as Nick's arm tightened round her slim waist. 'I'll have you burned by inches! I'll have you — '

'Quiet!' Nick ordered and, bringing round his other arm, he held the tip of the knife at the girl's heart. 'Just do as you're told, sweetheart, unless you want this knife in you — '

'You can't get away with this!' the girl

shouted, struggling again and kicking her bare feet against Nick's half-boots.

'I'm doing all right so far, wild cat. And I'll finish the job. First, tell these Redskinned scalp-hunters to cut Gamont loose.'

'I won't! I have given the order and — '

The girl felt the tip of the knife press tight under her left breast.

'*Do it!*' Nick hissed in her ear. So, nearly weeping with fury, the girl obeyed. The braves hesitated and glanced back at the elders — to receive grave nods. The safety of the queen was the only thing that mattered and her orders were unquestionable.

So the frightened, perspiring half-breed was released, his bonds slashed top and bottom. He looked about him anxiously.

'Start walking!' Nick called to him. 'If they shoot at you the queen here gets it. Go up the right-hand bank there where that rough trail is. You, too,' he added to the girl, giving her a nudge.

'I won't move a step from here!' she retorted, and he caught the defiant glare in her blue eyes as she turned to look at him.

'OK,' he murmured. 'But you're still the nicest and safest shield I ever had.'

And with an upward movement of his powerful arm he lifted her from her feet, holding her against him, ignoring the battering of her feet against his legs and the thump of her clenched fists into his sides.

Gradually, as the braves circled but kept at a distance, afraid for their queen's safety, Nick made his way across the expanse of stony floor in Gamont's wake. The elders turned and watched like so many models on a turntable, not a flicker of emotion on their hatchet faces. Nick wondered how long he could get away with it before it dawned on the Redskins that their queen was being kidnapped.

When he got far enough away he turned and walked backwards so that the girl was still held before him — then suddenly she shouted hoarsely:

'Shoot! Stop this escape! Shoot! If your arrows hit me I will forgive — !'

Instantly Nick dropped her. As protection she was no longer any help. He had one glimpse of her struggling to her feet in the dust, then he raced in a scrambling, tripping ascent after Gamont, who by now had nearly reached the summit of the sloping valley side.

Arrows flicked through the air from the pursuing braves, some only inches from Nick. He saved himself chiefly by moving in a zig-zag ascent, which made it almost impossible for the Redskins, skilled hunters though they were, to pinpoint him. And when they fired they had to stop to take aim — which delayed them. So, finally, goaded on by the girl's shouts, they abandoned their bow-and-arrow technique and instead plunged up the valley side with their knives drawn.

Nick kept going at a desperate speed, thankful when he reached the wooded region at the summit of the valley ridge. Gamont was ahead of him, streaking like hell amidst the trees towards a shining stretch in the distance — the River Maro, curving its peaceful way towards distant Texas.

Nick gave a glance behind him. The Redskins were still pursuing, dodging in and out between the trees in the distance, but, fast though they travelled, they were no quicker than Nick himself. He kept on going, panting hard, watching the river coming nearer.

Once he had gained its banks Gamont did not hesitate. He dived straight in and began striking out savagely with the current. Five minutes after him Nick plunged in too, the swiftness of the water bearing him away quickly from the Redskins who presently gained the bank, firing their arrows thick and fast — then when they found the two men had gone beyond range they dived in also and began to pursue with swift, muscular strokes.

'These Pueblos sure take some

shaking off!' Gamont yelled, as Nick began to draw level, swimming strongly. 'If they recapture us we'll probably get killed after what you did to the queen.'

'It was that or fifty lashes for you,' Nick shouted back. 'What are you beefin' about?'

Gamont did not reply. He kept on swimming, but with noticeably less vigour. The strain of running had exhausted him far more than it had the more muscular Nick. To the rear — and gaining — came the bobbing heads and sweeping arms of the Redskins.

'Better make for the bank,' Nick cried at length. 'Then we might stand a chance in the wooded country. We sure won't otherwise.'

He swung to one side, catching hold of the spluttering half-breed and giving him a hand. Broadside to the current it was tough going, but they finally managed it, emerging dripping and weary, with shingle under their feet.

Ahead loomed the forest by the river bank. They plunged into it, branches and twigs crackling under their feet, the vegetation becoming denser as they advanced.

'I guess I — I can't go much further,' Gamont panted, his legs staggering. 'I've gotta rest. I'm all in — '

'Rest nothing! Those Redskins are right behind us — Listen!'

Nick held up his hand sharply and, breathing heavily, Gamont caught the sound of distant crackling as the braves still pursued.

'Can't get away from 'em,' Nick said grimly, looking about him. 'They know woodcraft backwards and we've probably left a trail so clear it hits them in the eye — We've got to keep going,' he decided, and gripped the half-breed's arm.

Stumbling, pushing aside thick bushes, their shirts and pants torn by thorns, they kept going, hoping by some miracle that they would lose the Indians some-where in the labyrinth — but always, when they stopped for a moment, there was the distant sound of pursuit.

'Look!' Nick said abruptly, pointing

through the trees. 'Smoke! On that rise over there.'

Gamont peered through the leafy screen. Perhaps a quarter of a mile away, on a steeply rising ascent, a plume of smoke was curling to the cobalt sky. At the base of the ascent the wooded region came to an abrupt end and changed to rock.

'Trapper mebbe,' Nick said quickly, on the move again. 'Or at any rate help of some kind — Let's go. It's our last chance.'

Spurred by the thought of possible sanctuary, Gamont threw all his remaining strength into a last effort, and Nick, still gripping his arm, he sped beside him through the remainder of the vegetation and then began a desperate scramble up the rocky face of the incline.

'Hey up there!' Nick yelled, as he ran. 'Give us some help! Hey — '

He broke off and glanced behind him in alarm as arrows began to whirl towards him. They glanced off the rocks, landed in the dust — Further down the slope the Redskins had clear space in which to act, and were taking advantage of it. With yells of triumph they came speeding onwards.

Then, suddenly, the entire pursuit came to an abrupt end. From above there came the explosion of revolvers and rifles. Lead spat across the intervening space, over the heads of the two flagging exhausted men and into the midst of the Indians.

For a second or two the Redskins hesitated, and it cost them dear as four of them collapsed under the hail of bullets. To attempt anything against such murderous crossfire and on an open incline was impossible.

They began running — and vanished in the dense vegetation at the base of the slope.

4

Exhausted, Nick and the half-breed lay on the rocks, gulping for breath and watching three men coming down the slope towards them, their crossover guns slapping against their thighs.

In a moment or two Nick and Gamont found themselves hauled up. The half-breed looked at the men anxiously, wondering if by some misfortune he had run into another batch of Benton's boys — then the words of the tall, centre-most man reassured him.

'What gives, fellas? Run into Redskin trouble?'

'Yeah,' Nick told him, still breathing hard. 'An' thanks for the help. We sure needed it. No guns, no anything to protect ourselves.'

The tall man grinned. He was around fifty, hair greying over the ears. In spite of his surroundings he was neatly dressed in silk check shirt and black riding pants, with clocks up the sides of his half boots. Though into middle-age he was handsome in a hard kind of way.

'Best come up to the camp, boys,' he said. 'Plenty of grub and liquor there. You look as though you need it.'

Recovered somewhat and thankful for the respite Nick and the half-breed finished the journey up the slope; then as they came within range of the camp-fire they realized that quite an extensive base lay here. There were bell tents, cases of supplies, many men moving around — and nearby, corralled by ropes, were perhaps two hundred head of lowing, shifting steers.

'Starting a spread up here?' Nick asked, as he settled down and took the hot soup the tall man handed from the fire.

'Nope.'

No more information came for a moment. The tall man studied both Nick and the half-breed as they tackled the soup, then he said,

'I'm what you might call a cattle baron around these parts. Me an' my boys are tryin' to find a short cut through this dad-blamed Indian country for these steers. Somehow we want to reach Durango in Colorado where there's a guy waiting to buy the cattle. But this particular corner of New Mexico is so thick with Redskins you fall over 'em if you turn around.'

'You tellin' us?' Nick asked drily.

'Where's your spread?' Gamont asked, and in response, the tall man jerked his head backwards vaguely.

'Englewood — Southern Kansas. We've come a mighty long way with these steers — and we've probably an even longer one to go yet to reach Durango.'

'Not far off three hundred miles,' Nick told him. 'An' that's assuming you could go straight through, which you can't. The Redskins are between you an' Durango. Your only safe way is to go north to Purgatory Creek in Colorado then bear west right across the state to

Durango. An' I don't envy you in that mountainous territory.'

'Yeah, it's bad,' the trader admitted, rubbing his chin and thinking. 'We figgered on going straight through the passes in the Sierra Blanco, but the Indians are thick there we hear.'

'Thick is right. That's where we just came from — and did we have fun!' Nick whistled and finished his soup.

'What happend exactly?' the trader asked.

Nick told him in detail. When it was finished the tall fellow grinned.

'You sure were lucky to get away with it, boys. An' I'm glad to meet you.'

'Nick Carson's the name,' Nick said. 'I'm just a *hombre*, I guess, looking for the best thing I can find. This is Pierre Gamont — a general trader. Not exactly a friend; I just happened to fall in with him.'

'I'm Hartnell,' the tall man said, shaking hands.

'Most folks call me 'Slick'. If you want to join on with my boys you're more'n welcome. We can always do with a couple more.'

'An' do what?' Gamont asked.

'Try with us to find the safest way to Durango.'

'Across some of the toughest country in this part of the territory?' Gamont shook his head. 'Not me brother. You don't suppose I'm going to turn my back on untold wealth, do you?'

'Meaning that Indian town?' Hartnell asked thoughtfully.

'Yeah. As Nick here told you I got a lot of gold outa the place, thanks to whiskey — but all the stuff will have bin taken back to the queen by now, including my furs and wagon and horse, I guess. I ain't got a thing left 'cept what I stand up in. What kind of set-up is that for a man when there's more gold'n any of us can use packed away in that Indian reservation?'

'You must like punishment, fella,' Hartnell told him drily. 'I should ha' thought you'd have had enough of the Redskins without thinking of trying agin.'

'Not by myself I wouldn't. That was a tough matter. I was caught by surprise, same as Nick. We hardly stood a chance — But if all of us went — you and your boys along with us, I mean — an' armed to the teeth, we'd wipe up that town and everythin' in it. Then we could decide what to do with the gold and other valuables there are lying around.'

'Uh-huh,' Hartnell assented, musing. And Nick said nothing. His lips were tight, a glint in his eye.

'The thing's a natural,' Gamont insisted. 'First clean up the Indian town and take all the gold we can carry — then we've got a clear path through to Durango for these cattle of yours.'

'You figger there aren't enough Indians in that town to stand up against us?' Hartnell asked.

'It ain't a question of numbers, Hartnell. We've got guns and dynamite: they've only got knives and bows and arrows. Which is kid's stuff against us. We'd kill the lot of 'em in no time

— an' good riddance.' Gamont's eyes narrowed. 'Nothin'd please me better,' he went on, vindictively, 'than to have a chance to get even with that hellcat, Glorious Smile. I'd like t'do to her what she figgered doin' to me. Fifty lashes.'

'The dame don't interest me,' Hartnell said, shrugging. 'But the gold sure does. An' I think you've got something, Gamont. How's about you. Nick?'

Nick's only response was to shrug; which Hartnell took as acquiescence to the idea. He could not possibly know that Nick was thinking of the tempestous girl with whom he had grappled. She was white, altogether desirable, even if by some inexplicable process she was the ruler of a tribe of semi-savages. The thought of her falling into the vengeful hands of the half-breed was more than he could stomach.

' . . . So you agree, fella?' he heard Hartnell saying, and came to himself with a start.

'Huh?' he asked. 'Sorry, I was thinking. Agree to what?'

'That we follow out Gamont's notion and wipe out this Indian village clean. No reason why we can't do it — an' from the sound of things the gold's worth having.'

'Sure is,' Nick agreed. 'When do you figger making the raid?'

'Anything wrong with right now?' Hartnell looked at the men busy around him. 'We can get all the boys together in double quick time and then start moving.'

'I think you'd do better to leave it until dark,' Nick said. 'Plenty of those braves will probably be on the lookout even yet for me and Gamont — especially on the river banks. We've that river to cross, don't forget. No use making ourselves targets in the daylight. I'd say that about two in the morning is the time.'

'Okay.' Hartnell agreed promptly. 'Two it shall be. Until then you two guys had better rest up a bit — I'll see what I can do to give you a couple of guns and a cayuse each. You'll be needing 'em.'

★　★　★

Nick and Gamont spent the remainder of the day more or less idling about. Gamont was plainly full of excitement at the prospect of what he believed would be a devastating raid on the Indian settlement. Nick for his part said little. He had no love for the half-breed, anyway, had only helped him at all from a sense of duty — and now his duty was ended.

Nick did not trouble to analyse why he had decided to risk certain death in warning the Redskin Queen of threatening danger. It never even occurred to him that he was doing it not so much to protect her as to see her again. All through the day the vision of her lithe, angry form and untamed beauty hung before him. He wanted the night to come when he could be up and away.

It came, in its due order, and with the darkness the boys settled down for a few hours' sleep before the attack should begin. Everything was prepared for immediate departure, guns loaded, ammunition packed, all details attended to and a plan of attack mapped out. Nick had fallen in with the entire scheme with apparent willingness, but he took care to choose a sleeping spot a fair distance away from the next nearest man. He was pretty sure that if he was seen mysteriously vanishing from the camp there'd be awkward questions: maybe even a bullet. There was a look in the eyes of Slick Hartnell which he didn't trust.

Towards one o'clock the camp was completely silent. Nick lay fully awake in his borrowed blankets, watching the glitter of the stars infinitely high above him. Only the chill night wind stirred the vegetation and sun-cracked grass. It was the kind of night when perhaps the Pueblos themselves would attack in reprisal: Nick was constantly on the alert for such an eventuality — but nothing happened. It looked as though the Redskins had called off the hunt and considered themselves beaten.

Towards one-thirty Nick began moving silently. He sat up slowly and looked about him, feeling for the twin Colts that had been loaned him, and then the fully-loaded cartridge belt. Getting to his feet, he put on his borrowed Stetson and silently glided away to the cover of the nearest trees at the top of the rise. Here he paused for quite a while to satisfy himself that there were no signs of pursuit — then he began moving swiftly down the slope and presently through the almost impenetrable blackness of the woodland between the rise and the river.

He kept his right-hand gun levelled as he went, still unable to fully rid himself of the conviction that Indians might suddenly appear and destroy him before he ever had the chance to speak to their queen — but he remained unmolested.

He slipped into the river without a splash, his guns and cartridge belt wrapped round his head like a turban to keep them clear of the water. Refreshed as he was from long rest, he crossed the swift-moving water easily and emerged at the opposite bank, strapping his gun-belt back into position about his dripping waist, and still retaining one gun in his hand for instant use.

Alert for any untoward signs, he began moving through the deep woodland, cursing to himself as ever and again he inadvertently trod on a snapping twig or branch. The distance to the Indian town was not very considerable, that much he knew — but with the unavoidable noises he made he was afraid of attracting attention too quickly for comfort.

How right he was he found out a few moments later when from the density of the trees around him something suddenly whirred and settled over his head, dragging him backwards with strangling pressure. His gun crashed wildly as he fired; then it was snatched from him and he found himself pinned helplessly by three silent, wiry figures. His gun-belt was taken from him and, fiercely though he struggled, he found himself corded up so tightly he could hardly shift a muscle.

'So you guys were sneakin' around, huh?' he demanded; but he got no reply.

As far as he could tell there was a considerable party of the braves, dimly visible in the filtered starshine. Unable to move hand or foot, Nick found himself lifted, and he finished the journey to the Indian town on the shoulders of four braves on each side, being finally deposited in a crude stone building, the door of which slammed violently upon him.

Nick lay in the darkness and breathed hard. The only sign of light at all came from a narrow slit in the wall, intended as a window and far too small to permit the passage of his body. He had plenty to worry about, too. If the queen decided to make him wait on her pleasure Slick Hartnell would launch his attack and wipe out the entire place — which would probably mean the girl's death. It might also mean that Slick would find Nick here in the prison and draw his own conclusions — that Nick was a traitor.

'A rotten set-up either way,' Nick muttered to himself, and he set about a frantic tugging and pulling at his cords, only to satisfy himself that the Redskins were no novices at making knots. He just couldn't budge.

It seemed to him that an interminable time passed before he heard movement outside his prison door. He wondered for a moment if it might be the advance guard of Slick Hartnell's party which had crept into the village — then he knew differently when the door opened wide and against the starry sky there was outlined a girl's figure, her hair flowing and a blanket wrapped about her. Behind her stood the silhouettes of two of her braves.

She advanced slowly, saying nothing, and lighted a tallow high up in the wall. Then she turned and looked at Nick fixedly.

'You again!' she said finally; and Nick could not quite tell whether she was surprised or annoyed. 'When my braves described you I couldn't believe it — that you'd be crazy enough to let yourself get caught a second time.'

'I came back for only one thing — to warn you that this entire town, and you included, is likely to be blown skyhigh before dawn.'

The girl laughed softly. 'You expect me to believe that?'

'You've got to believe it!' Nick insisted. 'I've escaped from the gang who have planned to do it. It's Pierre Gamont's idea. He wants two things — your gold and your death!'

'At least you can tell a story, my friend,' Glorious Smile responded, her voice still contemptuous. 'Do you think for one moment that I believe it? That you would risk death to come back and warn me once you had escaped? You came back for only one thing — gold. As many a white man has done before. That is why I had my braves on guard outside the town. They captured you, and since you were such a fool as to play with fire, you'll suffer punishment — far worse punishment than before. You not only helped Gamont to escape: you dared to lay hands on my exalted person.'

'Right now I'd like to lay my hands on your exalted person again too!' Nick retorted angrily. 'Where it hurts most! Haven't you the wit to realize that I'm speaking the truth? You're doomed, the lot of you, unless you make preparations! These men have got guns, unlimited bullets, sticks of dynamite — They can blow the whole caboosh to blazes, and will.'

'Take him out,' the girl ordered briefly, motioning to the two braves, and she appeared to take no notice of Nick's shouts and protests as he was borne outside and across the stony ground of the basin. She stood thinking for a moment, however, and then motioned one of the sentries who had been on guard over the prison.

'Assemble a hundred warriors,' she ordered. 'Have them fully armed. Post them so that they guard this basin against all-comers. I have been warned of attack. Though I do not believe it, it is safer to be sure. If attack comes, show no mercy.'

The Redskin nodded and moved silently away. The girl watched him go and then moved across the stony ground to where Nick had been deposited.

'Because you may be speaking the truth, I have dispatched my braves to guard the town,' she said briefly.

'Good!' Nick responded in relief, looking up at her. 'That's more like it! I thought you were a girl with plenty of sense.'

'I am a queen, the ruler of this tribe — something you seem to have forgotten. If your warning should prove correct, I am grateful to you for it — but it can make no difference to your original crime, that of assisting Gamont to escape, and laying hands on me by which to accomplish your purpose. The elders will still demand justice.'

'Justice!' Nick nearly spat with contempt. 'What kind of set-up are you running here anyway? I risk my life to warn you of attack and you reward me with punishment!'

'That an attack is intended has not yet been proved. And your original crime remains unchanged. The elders will be severe. The lesson delivered to you is also intended as a warning to the braves, should any of them get the idea they can defile my person.'

'You're getting ideas too big for your sarong, Glorious Smile,' Nick said grimly. 'If you'd any civilized decency at all you'd not only reward me for warning you, but give me absolute freedom to enter this town henceforth whenever I wish.'

'I have to obey the elders, my friend, otherwise they can depose me.'

'Would that be such a hardship? You can't enjoy chasing around amongst a lot of Redskins, surely? With what you've got you could stand any civilized town on its ear.'

'At dawn your punishment will be decided,' Glorious Smile said coldly. 'By that time we shall know if you have spoken the truth concerning attack. I will do what I can to temper the justice of the elders because I am white — and you are white.'

With that she turned away, and Nick was left staring after her majestic figure as, the blanket flowing, she headed towards her own domain. He looked around him on the gloomy expanses, up at the stars, then finally at three Redskins not very far distant who were keeping an eye on him.

He relaxed, cursing the tightness of his cords, and waited to see what would happen next. He presently observed a Redskin coming towards him from the distance. True to his custom the Indian made no comment; he simply studied Nick intently for a while in the light, then he turned and strode towards the tent of his queen. The girl herself, relaxed amidst the furs of her bed, looked up with a start as the door-covering was pushed aside. In the bobbing light of the wall tallow the young warrior contemplated her dourly.

'Shining Fire demand full penalty for the paleface,' he said in an icy voice.

The girl sat up slowly, her eyes glinting. 'By what right do you, Shining Fire, enter my abode and make demands?'

'Shining Fire your tribal brother. I have that right.'

'Foster-brother, yes,' Glorious Smile admitted, 'but that does not grant you liberties. And the paleface is under my jurisdiction, not yours.'

'Shining Fire has power to influence the elders,' the young brave stated un-emotionally. 'Shining Fire will demand death of the paleface. He laid hands on the queen.'

The girl gave a contemptuous smile. 'That isn't what troubles you, Shining Fire. You have always hated me since we played together under White Cloud's guidance. You seek only my destruction, or else to take me as squaw. You are jealous of the paleface, Shining Fire. That is why you want him destroyed.'

'The paleface committed grave crime, Glorious Smile. He held you to him. Tribal rite say that is bad.'

'Leave me!' the girl snapped. 'When you rule, Shining Fire, it will be time enough for you to speak. Until that time comes I am your ruler . . . Leave!'

The brave hesitated, his immobile face looking as though it were carved out of teak. His dark, vengeful eyes studied the girl for a moment or two; then he turned and went, his steel-trap mouth shut hard. Glorious Smile relaxed wearily amongst the furs when he had gone. She was beginning to find her responsibilities mounting up on her. She knew too that Shining Fire only awaited his chance, to either marry her or kill her. Presumably he still had the belief that she would become his squaw since he was determined to remove what he believed was opposition.

Opposition? Glorious Smile considered this. Of course Nick Carson was a white man, and she was a white woman. Race must inevitably call to race, and evidently Shining Fire had been quick to grasp the fact —

Then the fur covering over the entrance way was whipped aside again. The girl looked up in annoyance, but it faded quickly as she saw it was not Shining Fire this time but one of the braves whom she had despatched to watch for an attack on the town.

'Paleface spoke truth, Glorious Smile,' he announced. 'White party came. We arrange ambush. Palefaces got wind of us and went back over river.'

'What's that?' the girl asked sharply. 'You mean you didn't get them? Kill them?'

'Went back over river,' the brave repeated stolidly. 'No paleface hurt. Palefaces may try again.'

'So they saw you in time, did they? Very well — keep guard against any fresh attack.'

The brave nodded and went out. The girl sat frowning to herself for a moment or two, then she got up and began dressing, adding to her sarong the trinkets and jewels which denoted her position of office. By the time she had finished dawn was showing through the slit window.

In the meantime, half dead with cramp, Nick was still lying where he had been flung. He had seen comings and goings, heard distant gunfire, and that was all. So far no attack seemed to have materialized. The only satisfaction he had was that the dawn was coming, which ought to mean action. He was commencing to feel that if he didn't restore circulation soon he would never be able to move again.

Then, as the first shafts of sunlight struck down on the basin he saw things begin to happen. Glorious Smile appeared in the company of the elders, the Redskin guards grouped about them. As on the former occasion she took up her position on the stone throne, the elders on either side of her, impartial in expression, their arms folded.

A moment or two elapsed and then Nick found himself lifted by the two nearby guardian Redskins and carried to a spot a few feet away from the throne and perhaps a yard from the whipping-post. He lay looking up at the girl's stony face.

'White man,' she said, rising to address him, 'it has been proven that you spoke the truth in warning us of intended attack. The attack was withdrawn. For that we are grateful.'

Nick didn't say anything. He was waiting to see what happened next. The girl looked to either side of her, plainly ill at case with the elders inscrutably watching her every move.

'Your warning to us has decreased the severity of the punishment it was intended to mete out to you,' she continued; 'but even so, you have still to pay the penalty for helping a criminal and laying hands on me when I could not defend myself. The elders and I have yet to decide what that punishment shall be.'

The girl sat down again preparatory to consulting with the elders, then she turned with dignified surprise as Shining Fire stepped forward suddenly from the serried ranks behind the elders-ranks which formed a tribunal.

'I demand death for the paleface!' he declared, halting in front of the throne and raising one hand in emphasis.

'Your demands have got no meaning, Shining Fire,' Glorious Smile retorted. 'The decision rests with the elders and myself.'

'My decision ranks higher than the elders,' the brave said curtly. 'Shining Fire is the son of the former ruler — the only surviving male descendant by blood.'

'But I am queen,' the girl pointed out.

'You are queen, yes; but my decision is still powerful enough to influence the elders. Shining Fire was only prevented from being ruler by whim of White Cloud. He loved Glorious Smile and hated Shining Fire.'

'He hated a coward, Shining Fire,' the girl said. 'That is why you are not the ruler.'

The young brave set his mouth for a moment, then he swung and pointed to the recumbent Nick as he watched the argument tensely.

'We have only word of paleface that he came to warn,' he said fiercely. 'How do we know he was not spy? Sent in advance? When captured he pretended he came to warn us.'

'If I hadn't got these ropes around me, Shining Fire, I'd kick your teeth out for that,' Nick snapped, in the tribal tongue.

The elders looked at one another. Though true to the queen White Cloud had appointed they had a more natural tendency to heed the words of one of their own kind. Glorious Smile noticed it and stood up again regally.

'Shining Fire, I believe you tell lies

and invent stories to discredit the paleface. I am satisfied that he came to warn us. Now go! I have spoken.'

'I go,' Shining Fire agreed, 'but I demand true justice. If the paleface only be punished and allowed to go free much woe will come upon us ere many moons have passed — and you, Glorious Smile, will be the cause.'

With that the brave went back to the ranks from which he had come. He knew he had made an impression — and so did Glorious Smile. She turned to the elders with a worried expression and began her consultation with them. Nick waited, wondering just how much nearer he had come to death through Shining Fire's vindictive interception.

Her argument with the elders was a long one. It was evident from her movements and the rising tide of anger in her face that she was not in agreement with their observations; but at last she had to give way. Very slowly she got to her feet and spoke in a voice

Nick hardly recognized.

'White man, for laying hands upon my exalted personage and helping a criminal to escape it is the verdict of the elders of this tribe, and myself, that you shall be put to death. The ordeal by fire shall pass you by, but death shall be dealt to you by one shot of the arrow, straight to the heart!'

'But — but you can't mean that!' Nick cried hoarsely. 'What kind of filthy justice is it that — '

'I have spoken,' the girl said listlessly, and gave him a steady look. He knew what she meant; that she was powerless to alter the verdict of those who formed her retinue.

'You're not a queen, Glorious Smile; you're a dumb figurehead!' Nick yelled. 'You're stuck up on that throne for these Indian sadists to do as they like with! You're a — '

'I claim the right, Glorious Smile, to release the shaft that shall destroy this paleface!' Shining Fire stepped down from the ranks, his sinewy hands already slinging the bow from his shoulder.

'I expected that from you, Shining Fire,' the girl told him bitterly. 'To shoot a bound man and kill him is all the bravery of which you are capable. Even the coyotes have more courage than you.'

'Shining Fire only carry out justice on paleface!' the brave retorted.

'So be it,' Glorious Smile said tonelessly. 'Prepare the prisoner.'

She settled down again on the throne, her face starkly worried, then sat watching as Nick's cords were unbound and he was dragged on his feet. So numbed were his legs he could hardly stand. He was dragged to the whipping-post and there secured tightly, double cords about his neck, waist and ankles and his wrists secured behind him. His frozen look of contempt made the girl glance away.

'Prepare,' she ordered Shining Fire, and with his nearest approach to a malicious grin he backed the number of paces prescribed by tribal law, finishing up perhaps ten yards away.

Nick watched the brave in fascination. He still could not believe that this was the end of everything, that the girl would let such a heinous injustice be carried through — His gaze switched back to her. She was not looking at him. Her golden head was bowed, one hand raised to her brow.

Then Nick saw something else and he stiffened abruptly. Not three feet from the girl, slithering in the dust, was something which he took at first to be a length of brightly coloured rope — then it dawned on him that it was a rattlesnake.

And nobody was looking at it! Nick forgot all about the Redskin just fixing his bow and yelled hoarsely.

'A rattler. Look out!'

Instantly the girl looked up, then stared in frozen terror at the sinuous length only a yard or so from her feet. Its vicious head reared, then Nick shouted again with all his power. Immediately, startled, the snake began rattling its tail, sure enough sign that it was too irritated for the moment to strike.

'Kill it!' the girl screamed, still too paralysed to move. 'Shining Fire! You have your arrow fixed — Kill this reptile.'

'Shining Fire kill only paleface,' the brave growled.

'Kill it somebody,' Nick shouted. 'Or else throw things at it. Keep it irritated with its tail rattling while the queen gets clear. As long as it rattles it's safe!'

Shining Fire hesitated, then he lowered his bow and arrow quickly and backed away as the reptile, infuriated and with tail quivering, swung its vile head round and looked at him. It was too much for the recreant brave. He turned and ran for safety, the eyes of the elders following.

Then from another of the braves an arrow hurtled dead to the mark, driving clean through the vicious little brain.

The snake relaxed on its coils, dead.

Nick found perspiration was pouring down his face. He waited and watched whilst the girl recovered herself slowly her eyes following the dead reptile as it was flung away with a stick. Then she got on her feet, turning to listen for a moment to the elders. Finally she motioned.

'Release the paleface!' she ordered.

The braves obeyed as promptly as when they fastened Nick to the whipping-post. His cords fell from him and he half stumbled forward, pins and needles surging through him. The girl waited until he had recovered, then he went slowly forward towards her and stopped a few feet from the throne.

'The elders are agreed, white man, that you are a strange creature,' the girl said. 'First you lay your hands upon me and escape; then you call in time to save my life from the snake. For that punishment is suspended.'

'Thanks,' Nick growled. 'I didn't rate it anyway.'

The girl's blue eyes strayed in icy contempt to where Shining Fire was standing some little distance off, his dark face grim with suppressed rage.

'Shining Fire has proven himself a coward yet again,' Glorious Smile snapped at him. 'He had the arrow and the bow but fled before the rattler. For that, Shining Fire, you shall be relegated to the lowest position in the tribe. One man alone saved me — the white. Had he not distracted the snake I would have been bitten, have died, in two hours.'

'You're not kidding,' Nick told her seriously. 'A bite from that thing would have finished you — and properly! Maybe that was what Shining Fire wanted, huh?'

For answer the girl stepped down from the throne and motioned her hand gracefully.

'Come with me, white man. I would have words with you. You have nothing to fear any more from my tribe. The elders have ordained that you be free, and it shall be so.'

Nick's eyes strayed to Shining Fire. 'I wish I could believe it,' he muttered. 'I'd feel a heap better with some guns to help me.'

'Your guns will be returned to you. Now follow me.'

Nick obeyed, ending his walking in the girl's own stone domain. He looked about him at the crude bed and furniture, the furs on the stone floor and draping the walls.

'Sit down,' the girl said, and settled on the edge of the bed opposite him. 'I want to make it clear to you that I was not in agreement with either having you punished or killed. That was the work of Shining Fire. You saw how he influenced the elders.'

'Uh-huh,' Nick acknowledged. 'I figgered you were having a stiff time of it, but when you gave way to the elders I couldn't help blowing my top. Sorry the way I slagged you back there.'

'You were justified,' she answered, her voice quiet.

'Just how much power has that guy Shining Fire around here?'

'Too much. He's my foster-brother, son of White Cloud who brought me up and made me queen — chiefly because he believed I had more intelligence than anybody else in the tribe.'

'And you — like this life?' Nick asked in wonder.

'I have never known any other. If, later, I grow weary of it I shall still be young enough to change my habits. To that end I have learned English and acquainted myself with the outer world through books and writings and maps.'

'Naturally your name isn't really Glorious Smile; that's only an Indian by-line. What should it be, if I met you, say, in New York or somewheres?'

'I do not know,' the girl replied shrugging. 'I have no clue as to my earlier life — beyond one thing. This . . . ' And she pulled at the slender gold chain about her neck and brought from her sarong a small locket. Snapping it open she held it forward.

Nick studied the faces inside — one of a lean-faced man with light-coloured eyes and a resolute jaw; the other of a woman who looked very much like the girl herself.

'Those are my parents — or rather were,' the girl explained. 'White Cloud gave me this locket when I was about ten years old and told me he'd taken it from me when his braves had brought me in from the raid on a white caravan. I suppose my people were killed . . . '

'And in return you've done your best to help these stinking Indians build up a town and form a social order — all derived from your own study and knowledge of books? You must be crazy. The whole filthy lot of them want stamping out! Don't you realize they are murderers?'

'Were,' the girl corrected. 'Three quarters of them are ceasing to attack the whites and instead are too busy with their own social development: that has been part of my teaching. But others, like Shining Fire, are still

136

ruthless slayers — and cowards at heart, as he is. I do not rule these people because I love them but because things just worked out that way and there was nothing else I could do. I've known no other life since babyhood.'

'Then it's time you did,' Nick said decisively. 'Say the word and I'll have you out of here in two shakes.'

'No . . . ' The girl shook her head thoughtfully. 'No; I am not interested enough in the outer world to wish to join it.' Then she changed the subject. 'You have a name? I have not asked it.'

'Nick Carson — wanderer, traveller, rescuer of ladies in distress. Interested in one woman in particular — you. In spite of everything you've said and done to me.'

'I said before, Mister Carson, that I did those things because I was compelled. How came it that you knew in advance about that intended raid on this town?'

Nick gave her the facts, only too glad to find she could talk and behave like a normal woman when away from the stone-faced dignitaries she served.

'Then, apart from wanting gold, these men seek a way through this territory?' she asked.

'Yeah, and for a very good reason. The sooner they get to Durango, the better for them. They're not cattle traders: they're rustlers. I soon found that out. The cattle they've got have the brands partly burned out and new ones substituted. Where the cattle have been stolen from I don't know, but I gather the master-mind back of the whole set-up is this Slick Hartnell.'

'So it would seem,' she agreed. 'And Gamont has thrown in his lot with these thieves?'

'Naturally. He's a card of pretty low order anyway — That is another reason why I warned you. He's itching to have your head on a charger, Glorious, and don't you forget it.'

'Thanks to you, the town is adequately protected,' the girl said; then she got to her feet, looking up at Nick as he rose too. 'I think you ought to know,' she added, 'that rescuing me has put you in a position completely reversed from your former one. You will be feted and wined. That is tribal law applying to anybody who saves a ruler or dignitary from death.'

Nick made a wry face. 'Couldn't I just be excused and be on my way? I've no love for this place now I've done my job of warning you.'

'You are sure you have no love for it?' she asked gently, and her wide blue eyes pinned him for a moment. He gave a grin and raised his hands.

'Okay, Glorious, you got me . . . '

'When you leave here you must be careful,' she added. 'Not all the men who attacked the town were killed: many got away. They must have noticed that you had deserted them, and they must also wonder how warning reached me quickly enough to create an ambush by my braves. Your life will be in danger from the very moment you leave here, Mr. Carson.'

'Yeah.' He reflected. 'You're probably

right . . . Anyway, I can take care of it if I have my guns. You promised them to me, by the way.'

She nodded and took the gunbelt and holsters down from a hook on the wall. Nick strapped the belt about his waist and then grinned again.

'That's better,' he commented. 'I feel kinda dressed again. Well, when's the feast? Let's get it over with, huh?'

'Not until sundown,' Glorious Smile answered. 'That is law too. There will he much dancing and you will be the central figure of honour beside me. In the meantime I will see to it that you have a meal, and afterwards you can rest. After that . . . '

She said no more. The future was uncertain. She moved to the doorway and then paused for a moment, her eyes sharp. Not very far away Shining Fire was moving. Nick saw him at the same moment and gave the girl a glance.

'Do you suppose he was listening to our conversation?' he asked.

'More than possible. I expect trouble

from Shining Fire before long, even more so now that he has been publicly disgraced in front of the elders for his cowardice.'

The girl watched him for a moment or two, then with a shrug she motioned Nick to follow her.

5

Slick Hartnell was not in the best of tempers. In fact he was in one hell of a rage following the repulse of his attack on the Indian settlement. With his men he was now on the opposite side of the river again, in the temporary base at the top of the rise where the cattle were corralled.

'It's pretty simple t'guess what happened,' Pierre Gamont said bitterly. 'That double-crosser Nick Carson slipped out ahead of us and gave warning. Can't be any other reason for about a hundred Redskins suddenly appearing.'

'Yeah.' Hartnell gave a slow nod, his eyes narrowed. 'I never did like the look of that Carson guy. Bit too smooth . . . Guess his idea was to try and get the gold fur himself.'

'Mebbe,' Gamont acknowledged, 'but t'my mind that's only part of his plan. I think he's got an eye on that hellcat who runs the settlement.'

Hartnell reflected. With the years he had not lost his belief that he was irresistible to women.'

'Wonder if I might make some impression on her myself?' he mused. 'If Carson can there's no reason why I shouldn't.'

Gamont shrugged. 'Yore welcome to try. Possibility is you'd finish up with an ordeal by fire. And anyways she isn't worth having. All she wants is killing, and if I ever get the chance that's just what I aim to do. I haven't forgotten she intended me to have fifty lashes.'

Hartnell got up from the rock on which he was seated. Hands in pockets he mooched around for a while, thinking, watched by the gathered, grim-faced men.

'I guess it ain't sensible to call things off this easily,' he said at length. 'An' besides, we've these steers to think of. We have gotta find the shortest cut to Durango. I'm all for making another attack on the Indian town. This time we'll be ready for any ambush.'

Nobody said anything. Gamont shook his head.

'I don't like it, Hartnell,' he said. 'These Indians know now that we might try again — and nobody can beat an Indian when it comes to shadowing and snipin'. I don't think any of us would survive a second time.'

'Then what the hell do we do?' Hartnell demanded, spreading his hands. 'There's all the gold we want in that settlement, and a short cut for the steers. I'm — not willin' to give up a prize that big just becos of a little danger!'

Gamont did not answer: he was obviously trying to think the business out — then suddenly he gave a start as his gaze settled on a hatchet-face peering at him from amidst the nearby bushes. He jumped up with a yell, snatching at his gun

'Redskin!' he shouted, pointing. 'There — !'

Hartnell swung round. The remaining men leapt up. Gamont got his gun levelled but he did not fire it for the Redskin came suddenly into full view, his hand raised.

'Shining Fire friend,' he said, in his own language and looked at Gamont

The half-breed hesitated, looking quickly about him for signs of more Indians; but everything seemed to be quiet.

'What does the critter want?' Hartnell snapped. 'I've a mind to plug him . . . You understand his lingo, Gamont?'

'Sure thing,' Gamont assented, and to the Redskin he added, 'Shining Fire be killed unless good reason brings him here. Speak on.'

The Redskin came forward and began talking in his garbled English, the men watching him narrowly.

'Shining Fire can show palefaces secret way into Indian town, under river. No attack against you. You in the town before any man knows it.'

'What kind of a tale do you call that?'

Hartnell demanded sourly. 'This is just another blasted trick to get us corralled somewhere in a passage and kill the lot of us. No thanks! All you'll get, poker-puss, is a bullet in your belly.'

'Just a minute,' Gamont said, raising a hand. 'There's an even chance he isn't trying to pull anything, Slick. I know Indians better than most, being half one myself. Look, Shining Fire, you offer to show us a secret way to overwhelm the town and your brother tribesmen. What's your reason for it? You do not love the palefaces as much as your own kind.'

'Shining Fire seek vengeance,' the Redskin retorted, clenching his sinewy hands. 'Glorious Smile she disgrace Shining Fire.'

'How?' Hartnell asked, irritated. 'What's all this about?'

'Glorious Smile disgrace Shining Fire and give honour to paleface stranger — Paleface Carson.'

Gamont's eyes slitted. 'Carson, huh? You mean that the queen has sort of

— er — become friendly with him?'

'Tonight he guest of honour at tribal feast. He save queen's life and disgrace me. Shining Fire seek vengeance. Shining Fire show you secret passage. You kill my tribesmen and take gold.'

'Sounds too simple to be genuine,' Hartnell muttered.

'You will expect some kind of reward for showing us this passage,' Gamont said. 'What is it?'

'Deaths of Glorious Smile and paleface,' the brave retorted savagely.

Gamont thought for a moment and then grinned. He glanced at Hartnell.

'Couldn't be simpler, Slick,' he said. 'This guy is so burned up over Carson and the queen he's willing to massacre the whole tribe just to make sure of getting those two. Which suits us fine. We can wipe out Carson and the hellcat all at one sweep.'

'Carson, yes,' Hartnell agreed. 'We'll talk further about the woman when we've seen her.'

Gamont did not say anything but his

lips compressed for a moment. Then Shining Fire went on talking, waving a hand to the nearby cattle.

'You seek quick way to Durango,' he said. 'Shining Fire heard paleface Carson telling Glorious Smile. These cattle stolen.'

'Who says so?' Hartnell growled, his face darkening.

'Paleface Carson know you rustlers. You bring cattle through secret passage. Turn cattle loose first into town — then attack.'

'That's an idea,' Hartnell admitted. 'These steers will sure cause plenty of trouble if we stampede them into the settlement. In the confusion we can take up our positions and give those dirty Redskins hell. Worth the loss of a few steers to gain an initial advantage.'

'After,' Shining Fire added, 'Shining Fire show you quick way through mountains to Durango trail.'

There was silence for a moment as the men weighed up the possibilities; then Hartnell's eyes flashed to Gamont.

'How do you figure it, Gamont?' he asked. 'Is this pokerface trying to pull something, or is it worth a gamble?'

'I think he's on the level,' Gamont answered. 'Even if he isn't we can protect ourselves by running the cattle ahead of us. They'll clear the path and give warning if anything is there. I get the idea that Shining Fire here is willing to do anything just as long as he gets his own back.'

'Okay, then we'll risk it,' Hartnell decided. And to the brave he added, 'When's the best time to get busy?'

'Night,' the Redskin replied. 'When the feasting and dancing begins. That will be hour after sundown. I return now to settlement. At sundown Shining Fire return to show you way.'

He raised his hand in the Indian sign of friendship and then vanished in the bushes. Characteristically he made no sound whatever. He might not even have existed. Hartnell took a deep breath and then grinned.

'Looks like things solved themselves,'

he commented, rubbing his hands. 'An' while we're about it, Gamont, let's get one thing straight. I'm running this outfit. Savvy?'

'Did I ever question it?' Gamont asked, surprised.

'No; but you're a bit too quick on decidin' what going to be done with Carson and this Indian queen. You want the pair of 'em killed.'

'That's what Shining Fire wants too. If we double-cross him and don't kill those two he might do just anything.'

'He won't get the chance,' Hartnell said coldly. 'The sooner we polish him off the better I'll like it. I'll find a way to wipe him out amidst the confusion: I don't trust a double-crosser at any time, an' a Redskin one least of all. Point I'm making, Gamont, is this: I'll decide what's to be done with this woman and Carson. To my mind a bullet's too quick and easy for Carson after the way he hogtied us. I may want to play around with him a bit at first

— As for the queen. Depends if I like her.'

'You're loco,' Gamont snapped. 'She's plain dynamite and as long as there's life in her she's liable to find a way of ditching us. Kill her an' be done with it.'

'Shut up,' Hartnell retorted. 'I'm running this mob, Gamont, and I'll do as I see fit. But for us you wouldn't be here anyway.'

'And you wouldn't have known about the gold,' the half-breed answered, breathing hard.

Silence. Both men glared at each other; then Hartnell relaxed and gave his easy grin.

'Okay, fella — it's fifty-fifty. Take it easy. I guess things'll work out right before we're through.'

★   ★   ★

Nick did not enjoy the tribal ceremony which began promptly at sundown. With Glorious Smile he was compelled

151

to sit on a double-throne carved out of a vast rock, and he did not feel any happier by having a garland of wild flowers placed around his neck by one of the elders.

In fact, the whole business seemed plain bunk to him. The only enjoyment he extracted out of it was being so close to the girl and having her as a friend at last instead of an enemy.

Out of courtesy he was compelled to drink the light wine which was provided and eat the meal which had been prepared. After which there was nothing else for it but to solemnly watch the festivities — the wild dancing of the Indians in the smoky, flickering light of torches and that of a giant fire in the centre of the basin floor.

Those Indians who were not dancing were either lying on the rock banks around the edge of the basin or drinking the non-intoxicating wine. The squaws moved about silently, looking after the children or else carrying food, the only two duties of which they seemed capable.

'And you mean to say you don't ever get tired of this life?' Nick asked at length, glancing at the girl.

Her eyes remained on the whirling, half-naked figures.

'Sometimes,' the girl admitted. 'You mustn't forget, though, that I have never known any other life, so it has a sort of appeal for me. Probably I'd soon outgrow that if I ever got to a city amongst my own folks.'

'Then what's stopping you?' Nick insisted. 'If you'll only come with me I'd very soon get you to something civilized — and with your looks and the way you've educated yourself you'd very quickly knock the folks' eyes out.'

'I think,' the girl said, 'that you should know that we have been put on this double throne for a significant reason. The elders have the hope that you and I will marry.'

'Yeah?' Nick looked astonished for a moment. 'Mebbe they're thought-readers. I've had the same notion for some time — I guess it's crazy, though. Only a short while ago you and I were sworn enemies; now we're talking of marrying.'

'I'm not,' the girl said quietly. 'That's what the elders want.'

'Then you don't think much of the idea? That it? You don't think I'd rate anything as a husband? I could prove you wrong if you'd get out of this infernal place and let me marry you in a proper way in a civilized town.'

'If marrying me is your only interest, Mr. Carson, why can't you do it here and become king?'

Nick reflected, his eyes on the dancers. Glorious Smile turned to look at him intently.

'You say you are a wanderer, heading for no place in particular. What is there to prevent you settling here? The tribe will always look on you henceforth as they do on me — as something sacred. All because you saved my life. They have a very primitive outlook, remember.'

'Ruling this lot of savages isn't my meat,' Nick growled.

'You wouldn't be expected to; I should go on doing that.'

'Huh?' Nick looked at her in amazement. 'You mean that if I became your king I'd just be your-your husband, and a back number, too?'

'I would still have the authority,' Glorious Smile explained. 'The actual ruler can only be named by the predecessor — as I was by White Cloud.'

Nick grinned and shook his head. 'Not for me, Glorious! Much as I love you I couldn't settle down as lapdog to a queen. I'm the type who gives his own orders. We'd blow up in each other's faces inside a week. No, the only way we'd knock sense into marriage is to do it properly, in a civilized spot. And I still can't figger out what you see in staying here.'

'I feel,' the girl answered slowly, 'that I'm doing a good job. I'm giving these savages a chance to become more educated. I'm crushing out their murderous instincts and making of them — within limits — responsible men and women with laws and society of their own. Other Indian races are doing it right now — notably the Algonquians. If I stay long enough I may live to see a race here which has become a model of excellence. In that way Red will one day mix with White.'

'In other words, the missionary instincts are at work?'

'You might call it that.'

'I might call it something else, too. You're too nice a girl to be buried in this dump. Try being Mrs. Nick Carson for a while in some town. If you don't like it you can always come back.'

The girl shook her head. 'Be too late then. That is just what Shining Fire would like me to do; he would automatically become the ruler by reason of being the son of White Cloud — and with him in power the whole tribe would go back to savagery.'

'Which wouldn't worry me a bit,'

Nick said, shrugging.

'You just don't see it the way I do, Mr. Carson. Let's leave it at that, shall we — '

Glorious Smile broke off suddenly, raising her head sharply and listening. Nick wondered for a moment what had attracted her attention — then he heard it also, the lowing and blatting of cattle on the move and the rumble of hooves on hard earth.

'What the devil — ' Nick jumped on his feet, staring around him, beyond the festive fire and the dancing Indians. Then he pointed to the grey wall of valley side nearby. Down it, dimly visible, there was streaming a herd of cattle, heading straight towards the basin.

'Stampede!' the girl ejaculated, astounded, also rising. Then she clapped her hands several times to make herself heard over the noise of the dance and the advancing herd.

'Better get these folks clear,' Nick said quickly. 'The steers won't go near the fire, but they can cause plenty of damage on the outskirts — '

He had no chance to get any further. A sudden tremendous explosion rocked the entire basin floor. It came from a point far above the animals, hurling rocks into the air amidst momentary blinding flame, and it was sufficient in itself to send the already frightened animals hurtling forward with added speed. In a rumbling mass of bone and sinew they came sweeping in the direction of Nick and Glorious Smile, perched as they were on the edge of the basin.

'Move!' Nick said abruptly. 'There's no other way out of this.'

He caught the girl's arm and hurried her forward. By this time the festival dance had ceased and the braves were dashing hither and yon, either looking after their own families or arming themselves in readiness to attack the raging horde.

At the door of the girl's own domain Nick came to a halt and looked about him.

'Nothing you can do with this, Glorious,' he said. 'Put yourself in this building of yours. The stone will protect you from the herds. I'll help these braves of yours get these steers under control. Looks like some kind of a reprisal by Slick Hartnell — '

He drew his guns and hurried away before the girl could say anything further. As he went he became aware of a sudden crackling of gunfire from half-way up the basin side; then not far away a group of stone dwellings vanished in white-hot flame as sticks of dynamite struck them and exploded.

'The dirty skunks,' Nick whispered, peering through the smoke and confusion as he looked for the perpetrators of the onslaught. 'First steers, then guns. Nice goin'! One of Slick Hartnell's specialties, I guess — '

He suddenly realized that the girl was beside him, gripping his arm anxiously.

'No use me staying in my own abode with these explosions,' she said. 'I might he blown to pieces. Sooner stay with you and fight it out.

'Okay!' Nick took her arm. 'Behind this stone wall is as good a place as any — ' He dragged her behind it and forced her down beside him. 'Can you fire a gun?' he asked.

'Gun or rifle — all the same. I should have brought my rifle with me.'

'Take this.' Nick put one of his Colts in her hand. 'Whoever you spot that isn't an Indian, shoot him down.'

'I don't need to be told that,' she answered viciously; then she ducked her head as another shattering explosion blew earth and stone skywards and tore up the distant whipping post by its roots.

Just beyond the wall the confusion was terrific. Animals and Redskins were mixed up in one hopeless agglomeration.

'I ought to direct the tribe,' Glorious Smile began, half rising, but Nick pulled her down again.

'No you don't, Glorious! Let the jiggers look after themselves. If you put your nose beyond this wall you'll never talk again. Unless I'm crazy, it's Gamont and Slick Hartnell who've pulled this trick, and their only aim is to destroy this town, you, and everything else.'

'But how have they done it?' the girl demanded, baffled. 'I still have an army of braves guarding every approach to this town. How did the cattle get here — and the men who brought them?'

'I dunno — ' Nick broke off, his eyes fixed on a gunman near the fire. The man was looking about him, ready to use his guns — only Nick acted first. His shot was dead true, and the man dropped heavily.

That seemed to start the fun in real earnest. The heavy explosions from dynamite sticks ceased and, instead, revolvers and rifles exchanged their onslaught with whirring arrows. Time and again bullets slashed at the stone wall behind which Nick and the girl were crouching. Now and again, as they caught glimpses of the invading gunmen, they aimed and

fired — sometimes successfully, sometimes not.

As Nick had known from the first,
there was no chance for the Redskins
with their bows and arrows against
guns, rifles and dynamite — to say
nothing of the still raging cattle,
panicked with the noise, who indis-
criminately trampled on white men and
Redskin alike. Even the addition of the
braves who had been guarding the town
— and had been brought back by the
noise of the explosions — was not
sufficient to hold the tide.

There came a time at length when
the shooting ceased and the braves,
beaten and divested of their weapons,
were trussed up securely in batches and
herded to one section of the town. Then
the cattle were rounded up and driven
into one of the enormous stone-walled
yards adjoining the cliff-face.

'Looks like we're beaten, Glorious,'
Nick murmured, as he watched these
evidences. 'The only chance we got
right now is for us to sneak away if we

can, before they come upon us — '

'You're sneaking no place, Carson,' a voice interrupted him. 'Drop your hardware — both of you.'

Nick obeyed, and gave the girl a warning glance to do likewise; then they turned to behold a tall figure behind them. He had evidently crept upon them unawares in his search for braves in hiding.

'So it's you, Hartnell!' Nick rose to his feet and helped the girl to hers. 'I figgered you were back of this business.'

'You figgered right.'

'How did you get here?' Glorious Smile demanded savagely.

'I should tell you,' Hartnell answered; then his eyes flashed back to Nick. 'This the dame who's been running this stinking tribe?'

'Yeah, an' if you start trying anything on her, Hartnell, I'll see that you — '

'Shut up! I'm doing the talking around here. Start moving, both of you. I'm holding a little conference over at the stone throne there. Looks like you're a queen no longer, sweetheart.'

The girl's only response was a frigid glare of her blue eyes; then she began walking, looking at the bound men and women of the tribe as she passed them. Their faces did not reveal what they were thinking; she could not tell whether they hated her for not having directed them in battle, or whether they sympathized with her in defeat.

Around the throne Hartnell's gunmen were gathered, probably two score of them, their weapons ready for further trouble. On the throne itself sat Pierre Gamont, at ease, grinning in triumph. It was a grin which faded when Hartnell spotted him.

'Get to hell off that throne, Gamont!' he spat out.

'Why?' the half-breed asked curtly. 'I'm more entitled than anybody to sit on it. But for me you wouldn't be here. You've run the outfit so far, Slick, but down here amongst these Indian lice I'm taking over.'

'Yeah?' Hartnell strode forward,

seized the half-breed by the scruff of the neck, then pitched him forward savagely. He fell on his face in the dirt and swore.

Nick and the girl looked at him, then towards a figure who had come forward silently from amidst the gunmen to the throne. It was Shining Fire. He held out his hand imperiously as Hartnell himself prepared to settle in the seat of office.

'Hold, white man,' he said in his halting English. 'Shining Fire alone entitled to throne. I give you free passage for your cattle. I allow all the taking of gold you wish — but I am ruler. Shining Fire has others who will help him keep tribe in order when you have gone.'

'Shining Fire!' the girl cried hoarsely. 'You mean it was you who betrayed the whole tribe to this — this paleface?'

'Sure it was,' Hartnell told her cynically. 'He showed us a secret passage under the river and into this basin. That way we kept clear of the braves guarding the town.'

'I — I never knew there was such a passage!' Glorious protested. 'Shining Fire, why was I not told? In case it might have been needed at any time?'

'Shining Fire exchange no secrets with woman who took his throne,' the Indian replied stonily.

'Which is one way of saying you're not wanted, Glorious,' Nick commented. 'Sooner you realize that savages will remain savages — and cut your throat when they feel like it — the better.'

'As for you, Shining Fire,' Hartnell said grimly. 'I'm going to sit where I please. Get away from that throne.'

'Shining Fire not allow,' the brave declared flatly.

'No? Okay. Since you've outlived your usefulness I might as well make sure where you are.'

Hartnell fired his gun twice in quick succession. Shining Fire stood for a moment motionless, the full power of his diabolical hatred expressed on his hatchet face; then he dropped slowly on his knees and finally collapsed on his back.

'Get him outa here,' Hartnell snapped, motioning to his boys. 'He's makin' the place untidy.'

Nick and Glorious Smile said nothing. The killing of the Indian had been ruthless, certainly — but they both felt that he had deserved it. The bodies of braves and women still lying about the floor of the basin were proof enough of that.

'Now,' Hartnell said, settling on the throne. 'Let's get one thing straight. I'm taking over here for as long as I stay. That understood?'

Nobody said anything — neither the distant-bound Indians, who were none the less in earshot, nor Gamont, who had got to his feet and was vindictively silent a couple of yards away.

'Okay,' Hartnell said, satisfied, 'I'm staying the rest of the night. Towards noon tomorrow I'll be on my way and those of you who are left can have your blasted town back. With us we're taking all the gold we can carry — an' we're taking our steers too. Where we're heading for is none of your business. You'll probably try and follow. If you do you'll get a run for your money. We're figgerin' to take a trail Shining Fire told us about.'

'There's no need to be secretive about that trail,' the girl said coldly. 'I found it myself years ago. It travels out beyond the valley here and leads through a mountain cleft to the direct trail for Durango.'

'Yeah — it would,' Nick commented. 'That's where these dirty rustlers are headed for.'

Hartnell shrugged. 'Okay, so I'm a cattle-thief and I'm heading for Durango. Seems I can't help you knowin' — But it won't do you any good. You won't follow, Carson, 'cos you'll be dead. You won't either, sweetheart, 'cos you'll be with me — An' as for these braves, the way they'll be nailed up before we leave it'll take 'em weeks to break free!'

'What was that you said about me?'

the girl demanded.

Hartnell grinned as he eyed her in the light of the still flickering torches.

'I said you'd come with me. It's the one thing missing from my outfit — a pretty face. An' you remind me of somebody I used to know many years ago, a gal I liked quite a lot.'

'You're not taking the girl anywhere, Slick,' Gamont said deliberately, coming forward. 'I demand that she be sentenced to death in return for the punishment she tried to give me. We've had this matter over before, and I still insist you finish her — and Carson too.'

'Carson, with pleasure,' Hartnell agreed; 'but not the girl. I make it a rule never to quarrel with women if I can help it. It would make life too dull.'

'I'm not going anywhere with you,' Glorious Smile said flatly. 'I'd sooner die right here where I belong.'

'You're not dying just yet, sweetheart — and you don't belong here either. I've got a place I'm taking up in Durango which will need a gal like you to liven it up. Golden hair, blue eyes, young; and just the right figure. I'm not too old yet to admire those points.'

'Why, you dirty — ' Nick strode forward angrily, his fist clenched, then he had to fall back as Hartnell brought his guns up.

'Take it easy, Carson. I don't want to plug you just yet. I want to make you smart a bit first. Seems to me there's something these damned savages enjoy called the ordeal by fire. Any of you mugs know what it is?'

'It has various forms,' Gamont answered deliberately. 'I'll explain in detail if you'll see to it that this hell-cat endures everything alongside Carson . . . Have you gone loco, Slick?' he went on furiously. 'If you take her along with us she'll do all she can to sabotage everything. You'd be safer with a tigress amongst us.'

Hartnell ignored him and looked instead towards one of the poker-faced elders standing nearby, his arms and feet tightly bound.

'What about you, wooden-puss?' he asked. 'What's all this ordeal by fire about?'

The elder made no response, and it was clear from his expression that no amount of 'persuasion' would ever break him down, either.

'I'm not standing for this!' Gamont shouted hysterically, whipping out his gun. 'This hell-cat's got to die — right now!'

He fired — but Nick had seen what was coming. He flung the girl down on her face in front of him, reeling himself sideways at the same moment. The bullet missed by a fraction; then Nick had twirled round and slammed his iron knuckles under the half-breed's jaw, flattening him in the dust. His gun, jolted out of his hand, bounced several feet away. Nick made a dive for it but Hartnell's foot descended on it.

'Relax, Carson,' Hartnell snapped. 'You're getting no hardware this side of heaven. As for you,' he added, to the fallen Gamont, 'get outa here! Go where the blue hell you like but keep away from my outfit. If you don't you'll get plugged. You've got the chance of staying alive as things stand — so get!'

Gamont rose slowly, his dark face venomous. Then, because he could do nothing else at the moment he got on the move, wandering away towards the spot where the Indians were secured together in groups.

'Do you think that's a good idea, Hartnell?' Carson demanded. 'He's half an Indian, don't forget. If he's so minded he'll release those braves.'

'So what? There's nothing they can do. Come over here, you!' Hartnell snapped to the girl — and when she made no move he gripped her arm savagely and yanked her to him.

'She comes with my outfit,' he continued, brandishing his gun. 'An' as far as you're concerned, Carson, I'm going to — '

Hartnell broke off with a yelp as Glorious Smile, still close beside him, swung up her clenched fist into his face.

Though the blow had not the power of a man behind it it was painful enough. Hartnell's eyes watered — then they watered still more as, taking advantage of the situation, Nick hurled himself forward, twisted Hartnell's gun-wrist, and flung him on the ground.

Then Nick dived. The mighty shove he gave the girl sent her sprawling into the corner away from the gunhawks. Things were happening so fast they were undecided where and whom to shoot. By this time Hartnell was staggering up. Instantly Nick closed with him, keeping Hartnell's big body between him and the prancing gun-hawks. The girl remained where she had fallen, watching intently, out of reach of the gunhawks for the moment. They, for their part, dare not fire for fear of hitting Hartnell instead of Nick.

Hartnell cursed as a smashing blow in the mouth turned his tongue salty with blood. Kicking out, he missed his mark: instead he got a blow on the ear. Nick spared him no mercy. He slammed and pounded with all his strength, until at last Hartnell released his gun. It bounced towards the girl and she whipped it up.

'Stand up!' she commanded Hartnell, and since he had no other course he obeyed slowly, dishevelled and bleeding.

Nick got up too, taking Hartnell's remaining gun and levelling it.

'If your boys start firing, Hartnell, you'll drop for good,' Nick warned, watching the gunmen narrowly. 'Glorious, go and release those Indians.'

Hartnell made an angry stride forward, then he stopped as the gun cocked at him. The girl, gun still in her hand, hurried away to the distant corner of the basin where the Redskins had been secured.

'Can you elders understand me?' Nick asked in the tribal tongue, looking sharply at the imperturbable dignitaries standing nearby. 'If so, take weapons from these men. I have their leader covered.'

Evidently the elders understood, for they began moving. The gunhawks swung round menacingly.

'Do as he says!' Hartnell snapped. 'I'll get plugged if you don't — an' without me t'lead you where are you goin' to be? You don't suppose this is the end of everythin', do you?'

'It is as far as you're concerned,' Nick told him.

The gunhawks had no time to make up their minds before their weapons were taken from them. Then Glorious Smile reappeared from the distance with a party of some twenty braves following her. At the moment they had neither bows and arrows nor knives, but physically they were ready for any emergency.

'Tell 'em to tie this gang of murderers up,' Nick called to the girl.

She did so. The men of Hartnell's outfit were seized and roped together swiftly, then dragged forward until they were in the centre of the basin. Here they were flung on the ground, a frightened, quarrelling bunch.

'Well?' Hartnell asked sourly, his hands raised. 'What d'you figger on doing now, Carson?'

'Giving you a fair trial along with the rest of your cutthroats,' Nick retorted. 'You've struck terror and death into this town, and the best people to deal with it are those who've been attacked. I'm turning you over to the Redskins.'

'With this dame as their queen?' Hartnell asked, glancing at the girl as she still held her gun. 'That makes it a cinch.'

'She isn't the queen any longer,' Nick answered.

Glorious Smile came over to him. He could see her face was surprised in the torchlight.

'But I am!' she protested. 'I have not been deposed — '

'Yes you have, Glorious. I'm deposing you, whether you like it or not. It's time you realized that you're a white woman, with all the responsibilities attaching thereto. What is more, if it came to passing sentence on these no-account killers your decision would be tempered by the fact that they are white the same as you. The elders will have no such considerations.'

'But I can't — ' the girl started to say; then Nick cut her short again.

'Listen, Glorious, I'm in this as much as you — and I don't intend leaving you in this place a moment longer than I can help. One day, sooner or later, you'll be mysteriously killed — if not by these Redskins then by some critter like Hartnell here. You're coming away, to a white man's town, and you're going to marry me. That's settled!'

Glorious Smile opened her mouth and then shut it again. Nick's sudden exercise of his male authority had left her pretty well defenceless.

'Do you elders object to my taking your queen, if she delegates a successor?' Nick demanded.

The frozen-faced retinue glanced at one another and then began to murmur among themselves. Before they had reached a decision, however, Glorious Smile herself suddenly turned and went to the throne, standing on the broad stone base in front of it.

'I am still the ruler of this tribe,' she cried fiercely, 'and the only way in which the white man can stay beside me is for him to become my king. I shall not leave of my own free will, and I call on all of you to prevent any such action on the part of the white man Carson.'

'Glorious, for heaven's sake — !' Nick shouted at her.

'My responsibilities lie here!' she flashed at him. 'When I go it shall be of my own free will. As for these men who have invaded us, I am as capable as the elders of giving a decision . . . ' She turned to the elders, exchanged a few words, then she continued, 'We are agreed on the punishment. At dawn the ordeal by fire shall begin, and shall end in the death of these interlopers!'

The braves murmured and nodded amongst themselves. Hartnell's expression changed and for a moment he looked genuinely scared. Nick looked at him; then at the girl. Finally he holstered the gun.

'Okay,' he said bitterly. 'Have it your own way, Glorious, but don't expect me to stick around as your lapdog. I'm taking a horse and quitting — right now.'

He swung away impatiently and the girl called after him pleadingly. He took no notice, continuing his determined walk in the direction of the town's animal reserve, from where he could collect a horse.

6

To turn his back on Glorious Smile was the hardest decision Nick had ever taken, yet his essentially masculine nature compelled him. The alternative was to marry her in name only and be forever under her dictates, which orders she in turn received from the elders of the tribe. Such a possibility to a man of Nick's roving, highly individual temperament was horrifying —

So, just as the dawn was breaking he began to get on his way. He was fully armed, bedroll and provisions strapped to his saddle, and a strong sorrel to carry him. He had half expected that Glorious Smile would appear to try and influence his decision — but evidently she too had more than her share of pride and refused to humble herself.

Nick's final view of the basin was of the flickering torch lights, the holes torn by the explosions, the Indian gathering in serried ranks to watch the ordeal by fire, and Hartnell and his men lying bound in one large party in the centre of the basin floor. At a remoter corner of the basin were the shifting, lowing beasts which Hartnell had intended to drive to Durango. The only person Nick could not see was Pierre Gamont, and the fact gave him a qualm of uneasiness. If any man was foresworn to destroying the girl it was Gamont.

At the top of the rise where he had halted his mount Nick sat gazing around him and wondering if, with Gamont being missing, he had a legitimate excuse for staying, after all. Then he shook his head. The girl had elected to remain as the ruler of her tribe: she must be prepared to guard herself.

His face grim, Nick flicked the reins and started the animal forward again, gaining the top of the incline, then disappearing over it in the dawn light. It was not long before he came to guardian Redskins but, recognising him, they let him pass with the sign of friendship.

By the time the sun was fully up he was well away from the Indian town and heading towards the sandy wastes which separated him from Des Moines. Reaching the town at noon he stopped for a while, then went on again.

It only dawned on him as the sorrel plodded on through the blazing heat of the afternoon that he had again become a complete wanderer — no responsibilities, nobody who cared what happened to him, the entire territory open to his exploring mind. A few days earlier he would have loved the prospect: now it rather appalled him. He kept thinking of a shapely girl in a sarong with golden hair and an independent manner.

'Quit worrying over the gal,' he told himself impatiently. 'It sure is too late to turn back now . . .'

He pulled his hat lower down over his eyes and peered into the blaze of the afternoon. It was time he forgot all about the delectable Glorious Smile and instead made up his mind where he was heading. It was not safe for a man to have no fixed course in these regions. He might find himself without food or water and miles from any place.

At the moment he was in Oklahoma. He had passed the State line not half an hour before. The position of the sun told him he was heading northeast. Well, that was not so bad. It would bring him eventually to Kansas — mebbe Dodge City, where he knew a rancher who'd perhaps take him on his outfit for a bit. Nick was quite surprised to find how he didn't like wandering any more. All he could think of was an Indian town and a girl who —

'Oh, nuts — !' he growled, and tried to push the memory of her into the back of his mind.

He did not succeed. As the horse plodded on gamely through the desert and then pastureland, following the recognized trail which led to Kansas, Nick kept wondering if the ordeal by fire had been carried out — if Slick Hartnell and his bunch of gunhawks had been wiped out; if Pierre Gamont had pulled anything to exact revenge. To all of these questions there was no answer. The only thing to do was to go on riding — and forget.

Towards late afternoon he was well into south-west Kansas, at a spot on the trail where desert, scrub and rock formed the only surroundings. A solitary water-hole tempted him. He dismounted stiffly, refreshed himself, and then lay down in the shade of the rocks. His horse, loosely secured to a cactus stump, drank at the pool and then loped into the shadow and began to nod sleepily.

For a while at least Nick found relief from his mental worries in sleep, but he awoke again to the realization that his shin was hurting badly. Opening his eyes he found a big fellow towering over him, a gun in his hand, his foot retracted to deliver another kick. He desisted as he saw Nick looking at him.

'Sure is time yuh woke up,' the newcomer said bluntly. 'Git on your feet.'

Nick obeyed slowly, keeping his hands up. A quick glance down assured him that his guns had not been taken from him — but from the look of the new arrival and the dozen or so men on horseback grouped around him there wasn't going to be much chance to argue.

'What gives?' Nick snapped. 'Can't a guy snatch some shuteye on the trail without getting a six in his ribs?'

The stranger gave a grave smile — He was around fifty, his face lean and bronzed, his eyes china-blue. From the look of him he'd spent his life in the open air.

'I guess yuh could have slept there for ever, 'cept fur one thing,' he said. 'That cayuse of yours interests me.'

Nick glanced towards his sorrel in wonder. It was half asleep in the late afternoon sunlight.

'It does? How come? Nothing unusual

185

about it, is there?'

'Only this — ' The stranger moved to it and pointed to the animal's flank. Upon it was a brand, half obliterated. The traces remaining looked like a double 'V.'

'Where'd you git this horse?' the stranger demanded.

'That's my business,' Nick retorted. 'Who in tarnation are you to get tough about the horse I'm riding?'

'I'm the owner of that horse — and dozens more, to say nothing of many head of cattle.' The stranger's lips tightened as he motioned to his dusty, sweating comrades with his gun. 'We're all of us ranchers,' he explained, 'and we're hunting down the dirty rustlers who've stolen our living from us — as good as.'

Nick said nothing. He was staring at the man fixedly; so much so the big fellow glared at him.

'What the hell are you gapin' at?' he snapped. 'Ain't yuh never seen a cattle breeder before?'

'Sure I have, only — You remind me of somebody, fella. I'm just trying to place you.'

'Yuh can do that later. Where did this horse come from?'

'It came from an Indian settlement way back in New Mexico. I guess I didn't know it was a stolen horse. I just picked it at random from a crowd of 'em and rode away on it . . . As to the steers and stolen horses you're talking about I think I can take you right to 'em.'

'Naterally — since yore one of the rustlers!' the man retorted, his bright blue eyes glinting.

'You got me wrong there, stranger.' Nick shook his head. 'I've bin mixed up with the rustlers, sure, but on the wrong end of the hardware. I found out their game and tried to ditch them; instead they got too smart and I had to move quick. Right now the lot of 'em are in the hands of Indians, waiting for an ordeal by fire. So I guess that takes care of them and makes your cattle safe. All you have to do is get your herds back from the Indians.'

'Yeah? An' yuh know where this settlement is?'

'I can take you straight to it,' Nick answered, glad of such a heaven-sent excuse to return to the company of the girl.

'Plenty about this I don't quite figger out,' the rancher said. 'Mebbe we'd better stop here for a bit and straighten things out. I'm keepin' my gun on yuh, fella, until I'm sure yore on the level in what yore sayin'.'

Nick shrugged. 'Up to you. My name's Nick Carson. No particular occupation. Just a wanderer.'

'I'm Grant Hansford. I own the Double-V ranch near Smoky Hill Ford — mid-Kansas. These fellas with me are neighbour-ranchers, all of 'em havin' lost somethin' and joinin' me in searchin' for the gang that done it. We tracked the herds' trail straight across Kansas. Right this fur, I reckon. Then we ran into you. I happened to notice that half-burned out brand on your cayuse, so I figgered I should have an explanation.'

By this time Grant Hansford had descended from his horse and settled in the shadow of the rocks. His colleagues made it their opportunity to rest also and began to disport themselves on the sand. For the moment, Nick noticed, Grant Hansford seemed in a more tractable mood. Even his gun was lowered.

'I like the look uv you, pardner, in spite uv my suspicions,' he said, rolling himself a cigarette. 'How'd yuh come to get tied up with these rustlers?'

'Just one of those things . . . ' and Nick went into a complete explanation. The only thing he held back was information concerning the gold which lay in the Indian town.

'An' this place is run by a woman?' Hansford asked in amazement. 'I reckon that's one of the queerest setups I ever heard uv. What's she like? Old? Young? Fat?'

'Young — an' a good looker.' Nick gave a grin and wagged his head. 'Just my measure, I reckon. Golden-haired, straight as a sapling, blue-eyed He stopped, frowning over a thought.

'Somethin' struck yuh?' Hansford asked.

'I was just thinking. Remember me sayin' you reminded me of somebody? I know who it is. It's the guy in the locket that Indian queen's got. Though I guess the guy in the picture would be the whale of a lot younger than you.'

Hansford's mouth opened a little and he swung round to look at Nick fixedly. Then he gripped his arm.

'Wait a minnit!' he breathed. 'What kind uv a locket is it yore talkin' about?'

'Gold. So big. Picture of a man on one side and a woman on the other — '

'Describe her!' Hansford interrupted tensely.

'Er — I'd say she was fair, with light-coloured eyes and a sweet smile . . . Holy cats!' Nick broke off blankly. 'What am I saying? The girl told me herself that the photos were of her parents, given to her by the Redskin chief when she reached ten years of age. You — you may be — her father!'

Hansford got on his feet in his excitement. 'I don't reckon there's much doubt about it,' he retorted. 'That locket is the one my wife an' I hung around the kid's neck when we hit the open trail fur California — just in case anythin' happened and her parents had to be identified. All these years I figgered she was dead — same as the wife. Your description settles it, Carson: I'll swear that that Redskin queen is my kid, grown up and ruling the very tribe which abducted her.'

'Soon settle it,' Nick said promptly. getting up. 'Let's be on our way. I'll get free passage into the Indian town for you: they love me like a brother. And by this time I guess Slick Hartnell and his boys will have been taken care of — painfully.'

Nick swung to the sorrel, then paused as Hansford gripped his arm. His excitement seemed to have changed to grimness. Hard lights were in his reckless blue eyes.

'What name did yuh use just now?' he snapped.

'Name, oh — you mean Slick Hartnell? He was the guy who ran the rustling gang, the one I've been telling you about.'

'Yeah, but yuh never mentioned his name till now. Yuh only spoke of Pierre Gamont.' Hansford clenched his massive fists. 'That's the dirty jigger I've been trailin' all these years, or tryin' to,' he went on fiercely. 'When the Indians struck he slugged me and ran off with my wife and kid. I heard later he'd survived but I never caught up with him. Now it turns out he's the low-down skunk who's bin handling this rustling game — '

'By now he'll be dead,' Nick said grimly. 'The Redskins and Glorious Smile were bent on that.'

'What are we waitin' fur?' Hansford demanded. 'Let's git on the move! This can't wait!'

Regardless of everything else he flung himself into the saddle and after a moment or two his colleagues got up hurriedly and followed his example. Nick, astride his sorrel, spurred the animal on quickly until he had caught up with Hansford's swift pace.

'We shan't strike the town until some time tomorrow, Hansford,' he said. 'It's around a hundred and fifty miles from here and across desert country for the most part.'

'We keep going 'til the horses can't go no more,' Hansford retorted. 'Like I said, this can't wait.'

★ ★ ★

Hansford kept up a pace which was killing, lasting well on into the cool of the late evening; then he was compelled to listen to the advice of his colleagues and Nick and give the horses a rest. They were no longer capable of carrying on without relief. So, much against his will, Hansford agreed to

193

camp for a few hours.

He himself was restless throughout the period but commonsense and the necessity for giving the horseflesh every consideration kept his impulses within bounds: but the moment the entire party of men agreed it was possible to continue he was off again at the same tremendous pace, Nick finding it hard to keep up with him.

By this time it was around three in the morning and the desert trail lay silent and ghostly under the stars and the light of the rising moon. Hardly speaking to each other the party thundered onwards, giving their refreshed mounts full rein, presently leaving the last of Kansas behind and continuing across the small stretch of Oklahoma which lay between them and New Mexico.

Once on the way they paused for nearly two hours; to hit leather as the dawn was streaking the sky. By sun-up. dusty and saddle-sore, they had reached Des Moines, breakfasting by a gurgling stream a little off-trail.

'How fur is it to the settlement frum here?' Hansford demanded, eating ravenously in his still unquelled excitement.

'Around a hundred miles,' Nick answered. 'And over pretty rough country, too.'

'We'll make it!' Hansford said, his jaws working. 'In fact, we've gotta.'

Once again the stay had to be protracted because of the horses, but towards mid morning they were on their way again on the last lap, Nick in the lead to direct the path, his heart singing at the thought of returning to Glorious Smile with a reasonable explanation to account for his return.

By mid-afternoon he was leading the party through the secret passage which Shining Fire had unearthed. Their feet echoing, and the horses being led beside them, the men walked through the darkness, their fingers touching dank and mossy walls.

'Yuh sure know your way around these parts, Carson,' Hansford commented. 'One mighty stroke of luck that we fell in with yuh, I reckon.'

'Uh-huh,' Nick acknowledged. 'And my knowing of this passage is a help too. It does away with the need to swim the River Maro. We might lose horses — and even men — that way.'

Conversation ceased again and the journey through the darkness continued. Having made the trip before Nick knew there were no clefts in the floor and the tunnel had no turnings, so it could not help but open up again finally on the incline overlooking the Indian basin.

It did. First as a distant star of light, then growing ever larger, until at last the men crowded eagerly into the brilliant sunlight and gazed over the town before them. Their expressions slowly changed. Nick, too, frowned hard, his gaze wandering very gradually over the expanse.

Nothing moved anywhere. There was no sign of men and women busy about their usual tasks, no smoke from the stone dwellings No anything, in fact, except a dark object here and there which might have passed for a body.

'What gives?' Hansford asked at last, his voice grim. 'Yo' bin' spinning some kind uv a yarn, Carson? If so yuh'll suffer fur it! This town ain't inhabited. Looks as it it's bin dead for years!'

'Must be some explanation,' Nick muttered. 'Let's take a look.'

He remounted his horse and rode it swiftly down the incline until he reached the valley floor. Then he looked about him, tight reining the sorrel as he jogged along. The dark objects lying about the basin floor were bodies, those of Redskins, the blood of bullet wounds dried on their corpses, their sightless eyes staring at the brazen cobalt of the sky.

Nick dismounted, drew both his guns, and went on an investigation with Hansford and his boys trailing behind him. In the stone buildings they got their biggest shocks. Here, still smouldering, were the remains of huge fires, and flesh. All the wooden furniture had

197

gone — presumably to make the fires.

In another building, one of the largest, half a dozen braves were hanging by their necks from the roof, stiff in death. In one of the yards four young squaws lay, nearly naked, their skulls smashed with savage blows. Nowhere an animal. The makeshift corrals were empty, and so were the stables.

One of the buildings had been practically destroyed by blasting, reduced to rubble, amidst which projected a solitary arm or foot where a Redskin had been trapped.

Nothing alive. Only the stench of burning flesh, bones, and wood and the quietness of death in the scorching sunlight.

'Well?' Hansford asked, his voice grim. 'What d'yuh make of it, Carson?'

'I just don't know,' Nick answered helplessly, looking about him. 'One thing is plain: this place, as a populated Indian town, has ceased to exist. It looks to me as though Slick and his boys somehow got free — then they drove their cattle away, as they had intended, taking the secret trail to Durango. They also took all the gold-bearing rock there was lying around here, as we can see from that shattered building there which was made up of gold-veined rock. Before they went they apparently massacred every Indian man and woman in the settlement.'

'Mebbe,' Hansford said, his blue eyes glittering. 'Seems ter me a mighty tall order fur a bunch uv white men to destroy a whole community, even if they did have access to gunpowder and ammunition. An' I'd say they'd be more concerned in gettin' on their way than destroyin' everythin' in sight.'

A cloud of dust swept across the basin floor, bringing with it glowing embers and bits of charred bone. There was something horrifying, inexplicable, about this funeral pyre that had been so prosperous.

'I haven't looked in Glorious Smile's

abode yet,' Nick said. 'Mebbe we'd better.'

He strode across to it, Hansford right behind him, the rest of the men still investigating the remaining buildings — and still finding evidences which sickened them.

It was plain that the domain of Glorious Smile had been completely sacked. The crude bed was overturned, the rugs tangled up on the floor. The rough furniture was smashed and one solitary mirror lay in a dozen pieces. Everywhere was confusion, the effect produced by ruthless hands searching for something. Of the girl herself there was, of course, no sign — no clue.

The life seemed to go out of Hansford at this point. He sat down heavily on the edge of the overturned bed and cuffed up his hat on his forehead.

'Looks like we came too late,' he muttered. 'My gal — if it *was* her — must be as dead as the rest of 'em. She might be just anywheres in this village, or even reduced ter ash and rubble. I still can't figger Slick Hartnell doin' all this, Carson. I know he's a tough character — a thief an' a murderer — but he wouldn't go this length. It's sheer massacre!'

'Yeah ... ' Nick bit his lip and looked about him. 'I wish to heaven I'd never quit! I feel I'm responsible for all this. I mighta stopped it.'

'I guess not. Whoever gave the order to do this wouldn't ha' bin stopped by you, fella.'

Silence. If the signs of disaster had done nothing else they had at least apparently convinced Hansford that Nick was on the level.

'Well,' Hansford said at length, getting to his feet wearily, 'I guess there's only one course we can follow — . We'd better try and trail Slick Hartnell as far as Durango and see if he did git away. I don't somehow think so, but — '

He swung round as one of his colleagues appeared in the doorway. His face was excited.

'Say, come an' take a look!' he exclaimed, and motioned outside.

Hansford followed immediately, Nick behind him. The entire party of men was standing around two of the dead braves on the basin floor, the two who had obvious bullet wounds in their hearts.

'Well?' Hansford demanded, coming up. 'What's so exciting 'bout two dead Redskins? We saw 'em as we came in.'

'Yeah, but — Say, Carson, did you say the Indians here were Pueblos?' demanded the rancher who had been talking.

'Sure thing,' Nick acknowledged. 'What about it?'

'This guy here — an' his pardner — are not Pueblos. The features are different. They's Aztecs.'

Hansford gave a start and looked at the sprawled bodies more intently.

'Yeah — yore right,' he breathed. 'In the excitement at first I never noticed — Aztecs! Hell, now I think I get it! The

Aztecs have been spreadin' up from the south fur long enough, shiftin' other tribes in front of 'em. It begins ter look as though some of them got this fur and wiped out the entire town. These two got bullets in 'em, which seems t'show that there was a fight for it. Mebbe Slick an' his boys were released to fight alongside the Pueblos against the common enemy.'

'Mebbe lots of things,' Nick said; 'but have you stopped to think what may happen to those taken away by the Aztecs? There's no guarantee that they destroyed everybody; and the traces we've found up to now all show it is the Redskins who've been burned and strung up. The Aztecs have a liking for human sacrifices, specially whites, to appease that deity of theirs.'

'Y' mean the god uv war — Huitzilo-pochtli?' Hansford asked.

'That's it. I never could get my tongue round it, though I've heard about it often enough.' Nick got to his feet urgently. 'I guess we'd better move!

Hansford, and quick! Glorious in particular may be in great danger. Nothing those Aztecs like better than a white woman — the better-looking the less chance she stands of avoiding becoming a sacrifice.'

'We can try and pick up their trail,' Hansford acknowledged grimly; then he motioned to the men around him. 'Let's be on our way, boys . . . '

No further time was lost in useless examination of the basin. Each man left the basin floor by a different route to examine the valley sides for a possible trail. It was Nick himself who finally came upon churned-up earth and the marks of numerous horses' hoofs and human feet. Immediately he signalled to the others and brought them to his side.

'I guess this is it,' Hansford said, looking about him keenly. 'Looks like a whole pack of horses and steers went this way — and human beings as well.' He squatted down and examined the footprints intently. Some of these belong to Redskins,' he said. 'They're distinctive — but there's a set here that shows a riding boot-fair size. What about Slick Hartnell? Was he wearing riding boots?'

'Uh-huh,' Nick acknowledged. 'Fancy ones. High-heeled with clocks.'

'Which means he at least was probably taken away by the Redskins. Don't see any sign of a woman's prints, such as Betty might have left.'

'Probably she was carried,' one of the men suggested.

'Anyways, the trail's clear enough. We'd best follow it.'

Hansford nodded and leading his horse beside him he went up the long incline, following the obvious trail. At the top of the rise the signs kept on going until they vanished in the thick woodland.

'We're followin' 'em, even if we go right across the darned continent,' Hansford decided. 'Come on . . . '

He leapt to the saddle and rode his horse swiftly down as far as the woodland, then he dismounted and began the slow, painstaking journey through the dense foliage and undergrowth, Nick and the rest of the men coming up behind. The trail was still quite plain to follow, and apparently had not been made so very long before. Saplings were broken, leaves still brushed back, rank grass flattened down. Here and there were signs of horsehair caught in the pincer grip of tree bark.

'No idea where these blasted Aztecs might be livin' right now, I s'pose?' Hansford asked, as Nick plodded carefully beside him.

'None. I never encountered 'em. I know they've been pushin' up from the south and given the Mayor plenty to worry about. But there my knowledge of 'em ends.'

'Might be just any place,' Hansford muttered. 'An' every minnit makes the danger greater — fur this gal anyways. For some things I'm gettin' to hope she isn't my daughter after all, just in case somethin' horrible happened t'her.'

'If anything has,' Nick said, his voice deadly, 'we'll destroy every Aztec we can see, and there wouldn't be anythin' I would enjoy more.'

The woodland ceased presently and they found themselves in the lower foothills of the Sierra Blanco range. Ahead of them, going to a height of perhaps two hundred feet, the trail of cattle and horses still showed clearly in the early evening sunlight.

'Wait a minit,' Hansford said, stopping the advance and contemplating the grey, impersonal heights. 'This may be where we start walkin' inter trouble. The Aztecs, like most Indians, choose a mountain retreat, so there's more'n a chance they may be packed away in them foothills somewhere. We'd better rest fur a bit and get our strength up, then carry on when it's dark. If they've got a sentry watchin' he'll spot us in this light and instead uv doing any rescuin' we'll probably find our guts cut out.'

The wisdom of his suggestion was obvious, though it was plain he found it a tough decision to make. So, hidden by the first towering rocks of the foothills, the party settled down and refreshed themselves and smoked. Hansford spent most of his time making sure his guns were in good order. Nick found himself watching the cloudless sky as the sun at last began to sink and the mountains foundered in gathering mist. The first chill breath of the night wind began to blow down from the heights.

With it there came something — sounds. Discordancies. Earlier the wind had been blowing towards the range; now it had completely changed direction it carried with it a barbaric music, a strange, disturbing chanting. All the assembled men heard it at the same moment and looked sharply at each other.

'Incantations,' Hansford said abruptly. 'Tribal dirge to a deity, and music t'go with it — sounds mighty like a gathering fur a sacrifice ter me. We'd better risk it and git on the move.'

He scrambled up with his men around him and they made hurriedly for their horses. It was not totally dark as yet but fast becoming so. When it did arrive it would be with the suddenness of a snuffed flame.

Hansford, one gun ready in his grip, set his horse moving. Nick kept beside him. Apart from the grim threat the distant wailing and music carried it also served as a guide. Then suddenly the night descended and Hansford gave a little murmur of gratitude.

'That's a big help,' he said. 'Cover our movements.'

He still kept his horse tight-reined as the advance continued. The upwardly rising trail was struck at length, a hardly discernible track of baked, trampled earth amidst the rocks, going up at its limit to two hundred feet. Half way up it Nick suddenly got a grip on Hansford's arm.

'Stop!' he muttered. 'Take a look up there.'

The men halted, motionless, gazing up towards a rocky promontory, perhaps fifty feet overhead. Against the blaze of the stars a lone figure was silhouetted, in the full regalia of an Indian, feathers clearly visible round his head and down his back.

'Sentry,' Hansford murmured, levelling his gun. 'Soon take care uv him — '

'Wait!' Nick snapped. 'The din of that shot will echo for miles in this space — '

'Not with that music and wailing going on.'

'We daren't chance it.' Nick insisted. 'Leave that guy to me. I'll fix him. Wait till I come back.'

He slid from his horse and sped up the trail before there could be further argument. Hansford motioned his men and they moved in silently to the dense shadow of the towering cliff so the watcher above, who had evidently not spotted them so far, could now have no opportunity of doing so.

Meantime, Nick had reached a rough section of the cliff face which gave him excellent toe-and-finger hold. He began climbing with swift caution, his eyes on the picturesque figure high above, slowly turning as he surveyed the landscape. Once Nick thought he had been observed and froze instantly to the rocks, expecting an arrow to suddenly transfix him but evidently he had been wrong. When he peered upwards again the look-out was gazing in the opposite direction.

Nick finished his ascent in a scrambling leap as he realized he could no longer be silent. He closed with the powerful Redskin before the brave had the chance to cry out or draw his knife. Exerting every ounce of his strength against the Indian's steel muscles Nick brought him down to the rocks, his fingers closing over the man's throat.

His ascendancy only lasted a second or two, however, then he found himself torn away and flung back savagely against the rocks. He shook his head dazedly for a moment, coming back to awareness as he saw the Indian diving at him with knife upraised.

Nick shot out his hand and gripped the Redskin's wrist, twisting it down and backwards with murderous strength until with a clink the knife fell to the rocks. Nick did not stop at that. He swung the Indian round savagely and then planted a terrific straight left in his face that jolted him backwards. Helplessly, he went reeling away, slipped over the edge of the promontory, and then disappeared. Down on the trail, fifty feet below, Hansford and his boys heard the body drop and saw the black outline of where it lay.

They hurried forward immediately to satisfy themselves. Once they were sure it was the Indian and not Nick who had fallen they kept on going, leaving the Redskin where he lay, his neck broken by the fall.

Meantime Nick had halted in his intended return to the trail below. His attention had been caught by dancing lights half a mile away and obviously at the base of a long incline — at the top of which he now stood. In true Indian fashion the settlement below was ringed by hills.

To descry any detail was impossible, but he gathered enough from the savage chantings to realize that some kind of tribal rite was in progress. He yanked out his gun and prepared to return to Hansford and the boys, but before he was half way down the slope to meet them they appeared, leading his own horse with them.

'Nice work, Carson,' Hansford commented. 'You sure took care of that Aztec.'

'Before he took care of me,' Nick responded. 'An' we've got a clear run to the Aztec settlement, far as I can see. I'll show you when we reach the top of the rise.'

It took them a few minutes more to gain it, then in grim silence they stood looking at the dancing lights of a torchlight procession. Other lights were stationary and were presumably torches jutting from the rocks around the valley floor

'Somethin' durned unpleasant goin' on if yuh ask me,' Hansford said at length. 'Best see what it is. We may run into more sentries, we'll haveta shoot 'em and risk the consequences.'

'Or knife 'em,' one of the men said. 'We've all got knives.'

'Except me,' Nick responded. 'Mine went long ago — but I've a good pair of hands. I missed getting that Indian's knife.'

'Let's go,' Hansford murmured, and nudged his horse gently forward.

Making as little noise as possible on the rocky valley slope the party began the descent, every nerve alert for sudden attack or the whir of an arrow. It seemed, however, that the Aztecs were not expecting to be molested for no other guardian braves were encountered.

At length the scene in the midst of

the bobbing lights began to take shape. Around the basin itself were grouped scores of Indians, men and women, implacably watching the scene before them. In the exact centre of the valley floor was a huge and hideous effigy — the war-god diety of the Aztecs, Huitzilopochtli. Around it, in solemn procession, marched the braves, carrying flaming torches, chanting as they moved, their voices wailing a barbaric song.

At the base of the war-god was a monstrous wooden lap, formed by the creature's crossed legs. In the lap figures were dimly visible, three of them, and from the appearance of their faces they were white-skinned.

'Looks like the real thing,' Nick breathed, lying down beside Hansford and peering over sheltering rock. 'Can't make out who's in the lap of that image. Looks like men. Betty doesn't seem to be there. She's only wearing a sarong so I guess her arms and legs would show up white — Yeah, men all right.'

'Time we acted,' Hansford said, drawing out his gun; then he froze as abruptly all dancing and singing stopped. There was not a sound for a second or two — then in one concerted rush — the dancers hurled themselves on the group in the effigy's lap, their knives drawn, their arms flashing up and down in a frenzied orgy of killing.

They did not withdraw until a different voice spoke, in the tribal language — a deep, commanding voice and probably that of the ruler. The braves withdrew, knives in their hands, and another procession of them appeared and removed the lifeless, bleeding bodies from the image. Nick watched intently and gripped Hansford's wrist.

'They're white,' he murmured. 'Only answer is they were probably members of Hartnell's outfit. Whoever they were they're finished now — '

Hansford did not speak. He was watching the proceedings below, his men tensely grouped behind him. Then more signs of activity began to be revealed as from the distant shadows three more figures came into view, held in the iron grip of the tribal warriors.

'There she is!' Nick said abruptly, and pointed to the slim figure of a girl being forced along protestingly, her hands held tightly behind her back. On either side of her was a man. In a moment or so it became evident that they were Slick Hartnell and Pierre Gamont.

'Wonder what they're figger on doing?' Hansford breathed. his eyes fixed on the girl.

'If you ask me,' Nick replied, 'all the rest of the gang have been disposed of and these three — central figures in the whole business — have been reserved until last. That's Slick Hartnell on the left — Gamont on the right.'

'Yeah? I wouldn't ha' known Slick again — not at this distance leastways. So that's my kid, is it? I just can't credit it, not after all these years . . . '

'You'll never get the chance prove it, either, unless we move quickly,' Nick reminded him. 'If we fire our guns amongst this bunch we'll be nailed before we can move a couple of yards. 'But mebbe there's another way,' he finished, looking about him.

Hansford did not appear to be listening. His eyes were watching the girl. Still held firmly she had stopped moving now and stood looking up at the hideous image, Gamont and Hartnell on either side and the braves gathered in a tight circle around them.

Nick gave her one more look and then glided away. He had spotted a brave not very far distant, probably a guard to judge from the manner in which he was detached from his comrades. In a matter of a few seconds Nick had come up behind him. He measured his distance and then sprang. He did not wait to use his fists: he brought down his revolver butt with savage impact even as he jumped. The brave crumbled, either stunned or dead, Nick did not trouble to find out. He snatched the man's hunting knife for himself and then relieved him of bows and arrows.

Quickly he made his way back to where Hansford and the boys were grouped, their guns at the ready. Down below Glorious Smile was evidently the central figure of the ceremony. She was standing now in the lap of the idol, her arms drawn back around it and securely fastened. Rope was also visible about her ankles and waist.

Nick squatted down, pulling an arrow from the quiver on his shoulder and fitting it to the bow. Then he stretched his powerful arm to the limit and weighed up the distance.

'I'm going t'do my best,' he said to Hansford. 'My idea is to get as many of these savages as I can to cause confusion; then we'll clean up the rest with gunfire. Have the horses ready for an immediate getaway. I'll grab Glorious if I can and cut Slick and Gamont free. They're not exactly pardners of ours but they deserve judgment in a clean fight, not amongst these dirty killers.'

'Yuh'll never make it to the gal,' Hansford muttered. 'Too big a distance. Arrows'll git you before yore half way.'

'It's our only chance,' Nick retorted, and continued watching as Slick and Gamont were hauled up to the image's lap beside the girl and bound securely into position.

Then the dancing began again, but this time it was plain no mere attack with knives — and ultimate death for the victims was intended. Instead, as the Redskins continued their crazy gyrations and made the air hideous with their cries, other braves came hurrying forward with stacks of dry brushwood which they flung at the feet of their three victims and piled up around the base of the idol.

'They're goin' ter burn 'em,' Hansford whispered, sweating. 'That's the notion.'

'Yeah. Mebbe a help too,' Nick answered tensely. 'The smoke from the fire will shield us to a certain extent. We've gotta take a gamble here,

Hansford, an' wait 'til the fire's lit. Then we act. Get the horses ready for a getaway. Put two men in charge to watch 'em.'

Hansford turned and gave his orders. Around the hapless trio and the wooden deity the brushwood piled ever higher — then at last the braves responsible for bringing it retired and the dancing grew more frenzied. Above the din of their singing could be heard yells of fear from Gamont, but none at all from the girl or Slick. Evidently they both had nerves hard enough to stand their fate without showing cowardice.

At a bass command from the leading elder the dancing ceased. That uncanny silence dropped. Nick raised his bow and waited. Then one brave went back a slight distance, commencing to swing his blazing torch up and around his head.

Nick's muscular left arm stretched to the limit; his right drew back, fingers just touching the feathers of the shaft. With a twang the bow straightened and the arrow flashed over the intervening space. It partly missed its objective and Nick swore — but only partly. The Indian with the torch suddenly found the fleshy part of his upper arm transfixed with the poisoned shaft clean through it. He dropped his torch and screamed.

Instantly the ritual and order of the ceremony was destroyed. The Redskins looked about them intently: the three bound above the still unignited fire moved their heads, obviously hoping desperately for rescue. Then one of the elders swept up a torch and flung it into the brushwood.

Nick permitted him to do that much; then again his fingers released an arrow. This time he made no mistake. The elder got the deadly sliver clean through his chest and dropped with a crash, the point of the arrow protruding from his back.

'Right,' Nick snapped, throwing down the bow and quiver and whipping his gun into his hand. 'This is it — Before that fire gets too big a hold.'

He dived down the slope into the midst of the now general confusion and smoke blown by the ignited brushwood. As he had hoped, the arrows from 'nowhere' had completely demoralized the Redskins, probably even more so because the elder who had died was their leader. The most heinous of all crimes had been committed: the chief dignitary had been slain.

Revolver in one hand and the hunting knife in the other Nick flung himself at the blazing brushwood, kicking it out of the way furiously. In the midst of the attack a Redskin appeared, took one look at him, then charged with his hunting knife whirling. Nick met the onslaught with a right hook, dropping his knife to do it. It jolted the Redskin backwards and a second afterwards a bullet tore through his throat and settled him for good.

Nick whipped up his fallen knife, plucked the blazing wood out of his path, then shielding his face he stumbled forward and gained the flat 'lap' in front of the image.

An arrow hurtled into the woodwork a few inches above his head; another thudded near his foot. He twirled, firing relentlessly at a few braves he could see beyond the raging flames. He thanked his stars he had allowed the brushwood to be lighted before acting: it acted as an excellent screen for his movements.

Three slashes of his hunting knife brought the girl half tottering into his arms. Without ceremony he bundled her over his shoulder and then cut Gamont and Slick free.

'Nice work,' Slick panted. 'I gotta hand it to you, Carson: yore a level guy if ever there was one.'

'Save the compliments!' Nick snapped. 'Follow me, both of you.'

That was not so easy as it sounded. The braves were dancing in furious anticipation beyond the crackling barrier as Nick — the girl over his shoulder — Slick, and Gamont plunged through the brief, roaring wall of flame. They ran clean into the waiting savages . . .

But Hansford had not been asleep either. Before the braves could wreak death or mortal injury with their knives and weapons a hail of lead struck them in the back. Hansford and his boys did not pull their punches, either. As fast as they had emptied the chambers of their blazing six-guns they refilled them, keeping up a constant barrier of death which gave Nick and the two men their one needed chance to break free.

They ran like hell, Nick stumbling under the extra weight of the girl slumped unconscious on his shoulder but the further they got up the valley side the less danger they were in because the darkness deepened. Down below there was still wild confusion, the smoke of the burning wood and image hiding the scene.

'Keep going,' Hansford yelled from further down the slope, firing over his shoulder as he went. 'The horses are ready — '

Nick reached the nearest one and

quickly draped the girl over it behind the saddle. Then he vaulted up and dug in the spurs. How the others fared was no longer his concern: they had as much chance as he of getting free.

He began flogging the animal down the opposite side of the rise, the wind cold on his sweating body, the stars clear overhead. It was only as the seconds passed and he struck the downward trail through the foothills and heard the hooves of his colleagues' horses behind him that he realized the rescue had been successful.

7

At the base of the mountain trail Hansford caught up.

'Don't slacken,' he ordered. 'Those blasted Redskins will do all they can to catch up with us — '

Nick didn't need to be told. He kept on flogging the horse urgently, one hand reached behind him and knotted in Betty's sarong to make sure she did not fall off under the constant jolting of the animal.

Without further words to each other, their whole attention concentrated on riding like the devil, each man rode his hardest away from the mountain range, Gamont and Slick sharing a saddle with two of Hansford's men.

By the time the woodland was reached there were sounds of pursuit, very far away; the rumble of dozens of speeding hooves on the hard trail.

Hansford glanced over his shoulder into the starlight.

'Let 'em come,' he snapped. 'Once we reach the woodland we can shoot the jiggers down as fast as they come up . . . In any case we can't go on at this pace.'

In a final mighty effort the horses finished the distance from the open trail to the wooded regions. Here the closeness of the trees and tangle of undergrowth forced a halt, anyway. Nick slid from his saddle, lifted the girl down gently and laid her in the thick grass; then he angled for position amidst the undergrowth so he could open up on the Aztecs as they came nearer.

Each man took up his position — except Gamont. He kept at a distance, crouched behind a tree, apparently plain scared. Nick had no time to bother with him otherwise he would have pinned his ears back.

In a matter of minutes the Redskins had arrived, their arrows whirling thick and furious into the undergrowth as Nick, Hansford, and Slick Hartnell too, opened up. From another direction the rest of the boys added their own fire, catching the hurtling braves in a sudden murderous crossfire which they had not forseen. They reeled and plunged from their horses, screaming with either pain or fury — but their numbers were such that they came on again in a second wave.

Time after time they tried to penerate into the density of the woodland, and each time met the crossfire which pumped into them without mercy. Their numbers grew fewer, their whirling arrows less numerous — then at last, beaten by gunfire and the position of the defenders they turned tail and raced away into the night.

'That oughta settle 'em,' Hansford panted, drawing the back of his hand over his streaming face. 'I guess the jiggers won't try again — or if they do we'll be so fur away they won't pick up our trail again. Best thing we can do is get back to that Indian town we started from. Plenty of chance there to fight if need be, an' plenty of cover. We've gotta rest somewhere, I suppose.'

'Good enough,' Nick agreed, rising stiffly; then he went over to where he had left the girl lying in the grass. She was just on the verge of recovering consciousness.

'How's things, kid?' Hansford murmured, kneeling beside her.

'I'll — I'll be all right,' she answered rather shakily. 'I just don't understand what's been happening — except that you an' Nick rescued me.'

'Sure thing,' Nick acknowledged, 'and you'll stay rescued, Glorious. This is Mr. Hansford — a rancher I've fallen in with. I guess he's got a particular reason for wanting to talk to you, too.'

'Oh?' The girl got to her feet with Nick's assistance.

'We can talk later,' Hansford said. 'Right now I think we should get back to that Indian town you were rulin' gal.

Nobody in it now, I reckon, but at least we can rest up a bit.'

A little distance off Slick Hartnell had started upon hearing Hansford's name mentioned. He said nothing immediately but turned away to his horse. Nick lifted the girl in his arms and put her in the saddle of his own mount; then he looked about him in the impenetrable gloom.

'Everybody here?' he asked.

Hansford looked around him. 'Yes, I guess so — No, wait a minnit. Where's Gamont?'

There was no response from him as his name was called aloud. The rest of the men took up the call, but only got the echo of their voices in return.

'Looks like he's vamoosed,' Hansford said finally.

'Can't see it matters,' Slick growled. 'That dirty half-breed ain't wanted, anyway.'

Hansford swung his horse round and started on the move through the woodland. Nick followed immediately behind him, one arm encircling the girl's waist. Further still in the rear came Slick, the darkness hiding the thoughtful look on his swarthy features.

'What happened?' Nick murmured, as the horse wound its way through the vegetation. 'I sure got one helluva shock when I got back to the town with Hansford to find everybody gone and a few dead bodies lying around.'

'It was a sudden raid,' the girl explained. 'The sentence on Hartnell, Gamont and the rest of them was about to be carried out when the Aztecs came. How they ever found my town I don't know, but I suppose they have all kinds of scouts scattered around among the tribes . . . Anyway, the only way out was to fight, which we did. I had Hartnell and Gamont and the rest of them released so they could fight with us — and they did. But it wasn't any use. There was . . . massacre.'

'So I figgered,' Nick mumured. 'We found everything shattered, some bodies hanging, and there were also plenty of signs to show that they'd stolen all the gold they could find, too. One of the buildings had been blown to bits and all the gold-bearing stone taken away.'

'Yes,' Glorious Smile whispered. 'They took all the gold — and every gem we possessed, together with a lot more gold that was hidden away. I was reserving it for trading later and trying to improve things.'

'Yeah? How come they got hold of all valuables so easily? I should have thought you'd've had everything nicely hidden.'

'They made me talk,' the girl sighed, as the horse kept plodding onwards amidst the trees. 'They knew I was queen of the tribe — and white into the bargain — so they didn't spare me any. I had to reveal all secrets, including information on hidden passages and so forth.'

Nick's arm tightened about her waist. 'What did those dirty skunks do to you?'

'Actually nothing — but their threats were sufficient to make me talk. I saw no point in holding out against them with all the tribe as good as massacred. Once they knew everything I was taken away with Hartnell, Gamont, and the others.'

The party was coming to an end of the woodland. Nick shouted ahead to Hansford.

'There's the secret way into the town around here somewheres,' he said. 'We'd better take it, save swimming the river.'

Within five minutes Nick had discovered it and, dismounting from their horses, the party made their way through its intense darkness, emerging eventually in the bright starlight over the deserted basin.

'All that's left of a thriving community,' the girl remarked bitterly, staring into the silence. 'You can't realize, any of you, just how I feel about this. I've spent my life building up the tribe — to see the whole thing end in massacre.'

'I warned you long ago this might happen,' Nick told her. 'The sooner you realize that your place is among the whites and civilization and not amongst Redskins, the better!'

'I've something to say about that, too,' Hansford remarked. 'Let's get down there and get something to eat and drink.'

'Better make it inside my domain,' the girl added. 'If we have lights visible outside here we may have to endure a second attack by those Aztecs. I can't somehow see them leaving us in peace after the way we beat them.'

Hansford set his horse on the move down the slope, the others following. Once inside her abode the girl quickly straightened the tumbled furniture and then lighted the tallow on the wall. Its dim yellow glow gave enough light to see by without betraying their position to an outsider. One by one the men came crowding in, bringing provisions from their saddle-bags.

'That's it — get it shared out,'

Hansford ordered, cuffing up his hat. 'We'll have to use water for drinking at the moment. Mebbe we can fix some coffee later.'

He ceased speaking, looking at the girl. Her blue eyes were fixed on him intently as she saw his features for the first time with any clearness.

'I know what yuh thinkin', gal,' Hansford said. with a grin. 'I'm like the guy yuh've got in that locket of yours, huh?'

Glorious Smile felt quickly at her neck, then relaxed. Like everything else of value, the locket had been taken by the Aztecs.

'How did you know about my locket?' she asked, moving closer.

'Nick Carson there told me — and I described part of the locket t'him. I s'pose it's a bit uv a shock, kid, but I don't just resemble the guy in the locket. I am the fella. I'm — your dad.'

The girl still looked at him, ignoring the sounds of the men setting out the meal, the scrutiny of Nick, and the grim silence of Slick Hartnell. Then suddenly the girl had her arms about her father's neck.

'Of course you are!' she kept on repeating, sudden tears in her eyes. 'I recognize every feature from the photograph. Older, of course, but then — I've grown a bit, too.'

'Sure have,' Hansford smiled, his bright blue eyes dancing. 'I knew some time ago you was Betty, my own kid, but there wus so many things t'do at the time I thought I'd tell yuh when you could absorb it properly.'

'I'm — I'm Betty then? That's my correct name?'

'You wus christened Betty — not Elizabeth — and the surname's Hansford. So I guess that wipes up 'Glorious Smile'. Though I ain't sayin' it doesn't suit yuh. Yuh sure grew up into one gal to be proud uv.'

Betty sat on the edge of the bed, pulling her father down beside her with a firm grip on his wrists. Whatever intimacies they discussed were not audible to the rest of the party as the meal was fixed up — but finally both the girl and Hansford took the food handed to them, and they were smiling.

'Feel any more inclined to quit this Indian business and be yourself?' Nick asked dryly, squatting nearby with a tin cup in one hand and hard biscuit in the other.

Before Betty could answer, Slick Hartnell spoke. His voice was grim.

'I reckon that makes two shocks for me,' he said. 'The first was when I heard Carson here call you Hansford; and the other was to find that this girl is your daughter. I never figgered anything like that had happened.'

Betty looked at him steadily, her face set. 'I haven't forgotten the way you descended on this town, Hartnell,' she said. 'Nor have I forgotten that you intended taking me away with you.'

'Yet you let me come here in the party?' Hartnell asked. 'I figgered you'd decided to let bygones be bygones.'

'You've been left alone so far because nothing else could be done,' Betty answered. 'We've had our hands full enough with other things.'

'Yeah, that's it,' Hansford agreed. 'But it's not goin' to go on that way. Hartnell. I've bin chasin' you fur years — ever since that night of the Indian raid when yuh slugged me and then rode off with Ruth an' th' baby — Betty here.'

'Yuh've no proof it was me who ran off with 'em!' Slick retorted.

'Nope, but it couldn't ha' bin anybody else. Nobody else would ha' wanted to shift our wagon and leave all the others standin' — an' I was durned sure Ruth wouldn't do a thing like that. 'Cos of that, Slick, my wife died 'an' 'til recently I thought my kid had gone, too.'

'I tried t'git 'em to safety,' Hartnell said, banging down his tin cup in emphasis. 'The Redskins chased us. Your wife got an arrow through the head an' it killed her instantly. There was nothing I could do, so I cut free a horse from the wagon and got away with it.'

'Leavin' the kid to whatever fate wus intended for it,' Hansford added coldly.

'I didn't have time t'think about her.'

Nobody said anything for a moment or two, and the meal continued. It was Hartnell who finally took up the subject again.

'Well, what's the answer, Hansford? You've caught up with me after twenty years. You've got guns and bullets in 'em; why don't you plug me an' done with it?'

'Because I don't shoot men in cold blood, that's why.'

'But you can't let him go free!' Nick protested. 'I've seen some of the things he's done — how he attacked this very town, along with that stinking half-breed Gamont. And what about the stolen cattle? Crimes like that can't go unpunished.'

'They're not going to,' Hansford answered. 'On the other hand we've

Hartnell's courage to take into account. He helped us well during that brush with the Aztecs; his gunfire accounted fur plenty uv the critters — '

'Only because he knew what would happen if the Aztecs won the day,' Nick put in. 'You can't paint Hartnell as a hero; he just isn't the type.'

'I don't aim t'do that — but out in the West here a man's fate is decided by his good an' bad points. Hartnell here is mostly bad but he has one or two good sides. Fur that reason I reckon that he should be given one chance — an' one only — to survive. If he doesn't, then it's justice.'

'Meaning what?' Hartnell snapped, his hand whipping down to his gun — but long before he could pull it, Nick had his own weapon levelled.

'Meanin' yuh should be turned loose in the desert with water for two days an' food fur one. No horse, no gun, no anythin'. If yuh can hit civilization in that two days yore a free man. If the desert gets yuh — well, that's it, I

241

reckon. An' if you do go on livin' yuh'll be a marked man in every State from there on. Yuh'll live quietly thereafter — or else.'

'What kind of a proposition is that?' Hartnell barked, his eyes glinting. 'All because you've got some crazy idea about my running off with your wife twenty years ago. The way things were she'd have been killed, anyway, in that Indian attack.'

'I'm not thinkin' about that,' Hansford answered deliberately. 'Fur one thing I can never prove what yuh did; for another I've got my daughter back, and twenty years has kinda smoothed the hurt I got when I lost Ruth. Yore being punished, Slick, for cattle stealing an' fur whatever happened in this town when yuh raided it. What yuh think yuhself, Betty? Is that a fair justice fur the critter?'

'Too fair,' she answered. 'Because of him many of my tribe were killed.'

'Not your tribe,' Nick said. 'You only ruled them by selection, not descent.

The Reds are not even remotely related to you. You've got to outgrow the thought that you owe them anything. If it comes to that it's the other way around. As for Hartnell here, I think that's fair enough, chiefly because none of us here is low down enough to do the thing we should do — put a coupla bullets in Hartnell and finish it.'

Suddenly Hartnell acted. He had been standing inactive, apparently listening intently to every word — but now both his hands flashed down and out, tearing the gun from Nick's grasp before he realized what was coming. Hartnell began backing to the doorway, his left-hand gun now added to his right.

'It'll take better folks 'n you to send me to the desert, or any place else,' he said grimly. 'I'll get out of the territory, sure — but in my own way and in my own time. The first guy that tries to shoot me as I ride away will get a bullet. Savvy?'

He reached the open doorway, then

suddenly he jolted visibly, pain contorting his features in the lamplight. Outside, the moon was now shining brilliantly, making Hartnell a clear silhouette. He jolted again, his guns falling out of his hands — then he fell flat on his face just inside the dwelling.

Instantly, Nick dived forward, staring at the two arrows deeply embedded in Hartnell's back. Nick turned and quickly dragged the wooden fur-frame across the opening, adding to it one of the long wooden benches.

'Aztecs?' Hansford asked quickly, jumping up.

'Looks like it.' Nick was on his knees beside the fallen Hartnell. He examined him quickly, then looked at the arrows intently.

'Is he dead?' Betty asked, coming over.

'Yeah,' Nick acknowledged. 'And these arrows are Aztec. Only answer is that they've followed us here — probably through the secret passage — and are somewheres outside. They know we must get out of here finally, so they aim to plug us one by one as we attempt it.'

Betty hurried quickly to the slit of a window and peered outside. There was a limited vision of the moonlit basin.

'I can't see anything,' she said finally — and Nick, who had just finished dragging Hartnell's dead body into a corner — gave a wry smile.

'Surely you've lived long enough with Redskins to know that they can become part of the shadows?' he asked. 'And I guess we can thank Hartnell for saving us plenty of grief. If he hadn't drawn fire to himself like that, any of us might have walked out and stopped an arrow as he did. Just as we still will the moment we poke our noses beyond the doorway.'

'In other words, a state of siege?' Betty asked.

'Looks that way.' Nick looked about him on the grim faces. 'I guess the Aztecs know from our horses that all of us are in here. They can wait until we break for cover and shoot us down in the doing; or we can starve to death here. By doing nothing they accomplish what they want, the destruction of their enemies.'

'They may be ringin' this entire basin, too,' one of the men said. 'We've not a cat in hell's chance of escapin', or locatin' them.'

'Bit uv a change from their living sacrifice stuff,' Hansford commented, frowning. 'I can't see a bunch of killers like the Aztecs just lettin' us rot here. They usually like t'see their victims die.'

'They tried the sacrifice and got a beating,' Betty pointed out. 'Or rather they did when they had killed all the men in Hartnell's outfit. Maybe they're not trying that again.'

'This,' Nick decided, studying the gun he had taken from the dead Hartnell, 'is a tougher proposition than it looks. We can't stay here to die — yet we can't get out without doing just that.'

He moved to the window and inspected the outside view as Betty had done, but nothing unusual was visible. Not that he expected it. The Aztecs had plenty of cover in the stone buildings nearby.

'One chance we might take,' Hansford said at length. 'Try and burrow under the wall of this place. What are our chances of doin' it, Betty?'

'No chance at all,' she responded. 'The foundations of these stone walls go down several feet. It would probably take days even with the proper implements. No, we'll get nothing that way.'

'Only one thing for it, then,' Nick decided. 'We'd better draw their fire somehow and watch from where the arrows keep coming — if we can. They won't be able to tell a dummy in this moonlight.'

'Any more than we'll be able to judge where the arrows are coming from,' Hansford pointed out.

Nick shrugged. 'We've got t'do somethin'. Let's try.'

He tugged off his shirt and stuffed some of the smaller fur rugs inside it.

On top of the rug he placed his hat — then the barricade was removed from the doorway and the dummy angled out with the help of a long piece of wood. Nothing happened for a moment or two; then an arrow flashed from somewhere and tore through shirt and rug with vicious force.

Another arrow came then another, at the end of which time Nick let the dummy drop and re-barricaded the door.

'Something queer here,' he said, pondering, as the rest of the party looked at him anxiously. 'Those arrows were mighty slow in arriving. I get the impression there isn't an army of Redskins out there at all, otherwise that dummy would have bristled like a pin-cushion with a shower of arrows. I think there's only one person out there — but he's in the position that he can hamstring us.'

'Gamont!' Hansford ejaculated, snapping his fingers.

'Right!' Nick confirmed, with a grim

nod. 'He disappeared from amongst us whilst we were in the wood. There wasn't anything to stop him picking up some of the arrows and a bow dropped by those braves we knocked off when they attacked us. All he had to do after that was follow us — and we by chance walked into a position where he's got the drop on us.'

'It's me he wants!' Betty declared, clenching her fists. 'Right from the very start he's been after me — since the time when I ordered fifty lashes for him.'

Nick looked about him and then made up his mind.

'I'm taking a risk on it being just him,' he said. 'I'm going out of that doorway with this wooden form in front of me. It will act as a head-to-foot shield and absorb any arrows. If our guess is wrong and there's a whole tribe out there, nothing can save me. But I've gotta know.'

Nobody argued with him because it was obviously the only way out of the situation. Nick gripped the tipped-up wooden bench in front of the door, held it by its inside struts, and then ventured outside. After a moment or two an arrow flashed from somewhere and thudded into the woodwork.

Nick grinned to himself and kept on going. When the second arrow came he fancied he had some idea of the direction of flight; and when the third one came he fired three times straight ahead of him, the noise of the shots crashing into the silent night.

The arrows ceased. Nick peered cautiously round the edge of the bench, but failed to see any signs of his attacker. He began to advance again; then his quick ears caught the rustling of the dry grass on the valley side nearby. For a split second he saw a dark object moving quickly; instantly he levelled his gun and fired two shots. There was no answering cry that might have indicated he had hit the mark.

Instead, an arrow flashed close beside his head and landed in the dust. He was satisfied now, however, that he was only dealing with one man — probably Gamont — and not an army. Risking everything he suddenly flung the bench down and ran like hell towards the long grass and scrub on the valley side, pinning all his hopes on being such a fast moving target in the moonlight no arrow would reach him.

His gamble worked. He dropped flat in the grass, breathing hard and listening. It was not long before he heard the rustling which denoted movement by his attacker. Nick shifted position slightly, both his guns ready, his body's weight supported by his elbows — then he jumped as an arrow, which must have been fired at random, thumped into the ground not a foot away.

He fired the one remaining shot in his right gun — then let hell loose with his left. At the same time he got up and advanced at a crouching run. The sixth shot of his remaining gun had gone when he realized every bullet had

251

missed. Instead, he was facing a dim figure with his bow ready. Nick did the only thing he could; he threw his gun with savage force. It hit his attacker clean in the face and he toppled over with a grunt of pain.

Then Nick was upon him, hammering at him ruthlessly with his big fists. There was little he needed to do, however, for the blow from the gun had already done its work. Pierre Gamont lay gasping with pain in the moonlight, blood streaming from a laceration on his cheek.

'Smart, huh?' Nick asked him savagely, flinging away the bow and arrow quiver. 'Not smart enough, though. You'd have done better to use your guns! Mind if I take 'em?'

'Smarter than you, anyways,' Gamont panted, rising up a little. 'I didn't fire because those Aztecs are on the search. They'll have sure heard the shots you pumped at me.'

Nick was silent, furious with himself. He had overlooked the possibility of returning Aztecs for the moment.

'Get on your feet, you dirty skunk,' he snapped, dragging the half-breed up by the collar of his shirt. 'If it's a fight you want to pick you can have it — right now.'

'OK, OK, you win,' Gamont growled, dabbing his kerchief against his cheek. 'I figgered I'd got th' lot of you beaten — an' that infernal dame in partic — '

Gamont flattened on his back, dazed, slammed there by a savage right to the jaw.

'I'm not lettin' scum like you speak of Betty like that,' Nick explained fiercely.

'Betty, huh?' Gamont fingered his jaw. 'So that's her name? When did you find that out?'

'Shut up and get on your feet again. You're coming right back with me, Gamont, to see what the folks think should be done with a rat like you. Hartnell's already been taken care of. You got him with your arrows.'

'Good,' Gamont returned sourly, a

hand to his aching face. 'He was a no-account buzzard anyway — '

He broke off and swung to look at the valley skyline, Nick doing likewise, as the silence of the night was suddenly split with a chorus of blood-curdling yells and the rumble of countless horses and running men.

'Hell — the Aztecs!' Nick gulped. 'They must have come to see who fired those shots — '

He didn't wait for Gamont — whom he had completely disarmed. His only thought was for those he had left behind in the stone dwelling. As fast as he could run he pelted through the dust and scrub, fully expecting an arrow in his back every second. Evidently, the moonlight and his speed made him an uncertain target, however, for he reached the dwelling without harm. Blundering inside it, he whipped up the nearest bench and jammed it across the door opening.

'The bed, too,' he panted, motioning hastily.

'Was it — the Aztecs?' Betty asked. 'We heard yelling. Yes, there it is again!'

'My fault,' Nick said, helping to lever the heavy bed in position as a barrier. 'My gunshots led them here. It was Gamont out there. I hadn't time to bring him here and decide what to do with him. I guess these jiggers will finish him, anyway.'

But in that assumption he was wrong. The Aztecs came upon the half-breed as he was deciding what to do to try and escape. In a few seconds ropes were around him and he was half-carried and half-dragged to the basin floor, secure in the midst of some three-score braves armed with torches and full array of fighting weapons.

'You talk language of whites?' snapped the leader, a hawk-nosed giant with an imposing array of feathers, and evidently newly-elected.

'I talk with all tribes,' Gamont answered quickly, sensing he had a chance if he assisted. 'Pueblos, Iroquois, Aztecs — '

255

'Silence! Do you speak language of whites?'

'I do — yes.'

'You will interpret,' the new chief commanded, and descended from his horse. Then with an iron grip on the shaking Gamont's arm he led him across to within a few yards of the stone domain. The Redskin was too wary to put himself in direct range of the window-slit. He kept himself at an oblique angle — to the fury of those within the building.

'What do you desire I — should say?' Gamont asked uncertainly, as the chief brooded in the moonlight.

'Tell whites we demand the woman for sacrifice. Our gods are angry that they were cheated of the ashes of her bones.'

'They'll never do it,' Gamont answered flatly. 'And the first one of you that dares to try and get in there will be shot dead. I happen to know they've plenty of ammunition.'

The Redskins, who had assembled

about their chief, looked at one another in the torchlight.

'The half-brother here talks too much,' one of them growled.

'Tell them,' the chief resumed, 'that for white woman we will give freedom to the others.'

'It's a waste of time,' Gamont snapped.

'I have spoken,' the chief retorted, slapping the half-breed hard across the face. 'If the woman can be got without my losing many brothers it shall be done. If not — we strike.' And he folded his arms and waited.

Gamont hesitated, then he went forward — raising his hands so the watchers inside could see he was unarmed. He stopped at the window and transmitted the message in plain English, but he added a few words more.

' . . . And there'll be about sixty or seventy of 'em out here. You don't stand a chance.'

'You hope!' came Nick's sour response.

'Tell that Indian big-shot to jump up a tree! He can't get at us in here, and anybody who tries it'll have their damned head blown off! He can't do it with fire, either. It wouldn't have any effect on this stone. An' if you think you can get in here with us, Gamont, think again. I guess Redskins are about the only fit company for you.'

Gamont returned slowly to where the Indians waited. Impassive, they listened to his report of Nick's flat refusal to comply.

'You try again,' the chief stated calmly.

'But I just told you — '

'Silence! I am satisfied that whites will not shoot you for mere words. This time you will act. You will enter by door, taking this with you.'

Gamont gave a start as he saw it was a stick of dynamite which had been handed to him. He held it gingerly.

'White men had much thunder stick,' the Redskin explained, evidently refer-ring to the explosive which had been in

Hartnell's outfit. 'We take. Useful — like now. Go in dwelling. Get girl out and kill others.'

'But I'll be killed myself!' Gamont cried hoarsely. 'When I throw this thing I'll go up with it.'

'Obey!' the Redskin commanded. 'We wait. If white woman not sent out quickly we follow you and kill. You have chance to escape thunder stick by leap outside. No chance if we shoot arrow in back.'

Gamont could do nothing but obey. Holding the deadly stick in his hand he kicked savagely on the barrier of the dwelling doorway.

'You're wasting your time, Gamont,' came Nick's grim voice.

'You've got to listen to me,' he insisted. 'I've talked the chief round. He's prepared to do a deal in these horses of yours. They're as valuable as a sacrifice around these parts. At least, let me in and hear the plan.'

Inside the dwelling the party looked at each other sharply.

'He's lying,' Betty said curtly. 'No Aztec would trade horseflesh for sacrifices!'

'May be some kind of plan, though,' Hansford argued. 'I guess we oughta let him in. If it's a trick we can fire fast enough.'

Nick gave a shrug, and with the rest of the men helping him he moved the barrier a little to one side. Gamont squeezed his way in, his lean face tense, dried blood smearing his right cheek.

'Now's your chance,' he breathed. 'Here — this is dynamite. My job is to blow the lot of you to Hades after the girl's been sent outside. The better idea is to throw this damned stick at the Redskins. We'll be protected in here. If I throw sideways out of this window I know just where they are.'

'What's the idea?' Nick demanded suspiciously, his loaded guns at the ready. 'You turnin' lily-white all of a sudden?'

'Nope. I hate the sight of the lot of you — and this dame most of all; but I hate the Aztecs a durned lot more! Mebbe I can level things out a bit by takin' a chance — '

Several things happened at once. Gamont dived for the window, the dynamite in his fist, just as the barrier crashed aside before two Aztecs. Evidently suspicious of the long delay they had decided to act. Nick fired point-blank and dropped the pair of them in their tracks; then Gamont hurled his stick of explosive from an oblique angle.

The report from it was terrific as it struck the rocky ground only a few yards from where the Aztec chief and his henchman stood waiting. Three of them dropped, killed instantly. Another one was literally blown to pieces. The chief himself was flung flat on his face and hammered with flying stone, but otherwise he escaped injury.

In the girl's dwelling the effect was cataclysmic, mainly because the barrier was away from the door. Hot air and a blast of dust hurtled in on the party, flinging the heavy wooden barrier before it. Tangled and struggling, all the men and Betty were flung off their feet.

Gamont was the only one clear, being out of direct line. He darted for the door in a last chance to make a getaway in the confusion. In one sense he was right. The chief and half-a-dozen Redskins plunged forward at the identical second. Gamont had one glimpse of a hunting knife flashing in the torchlight, then it buried itself to the hilt in his heart. He dropped, lifeless, and naked feet spurned him away into the dust.

Long before Nick, Hansford or Betty herself could disentangle themselves from the fallen barrier and tumbled furs they were being dragged up separately, their weapons taken from them, the hands of the Aztecs showing no mercy. Betty, Nick and Hansford were bound about the wrists and led outside. The remainder of the men were tied in one group, carried out of the dwelling, and dumped by its doorway.

'I guess that wasn't such a good idea,' Nick muttered, as he stood next to Hansford and the Redskins conferred with each other.

'Yore right,' Hansford acknowledged, straining helplessly at the twine securing his wrists. 'After the things we've done these Aztecs won't show us any mercy. I'm not so worried for myself, it's Betty I'm thinkin' uv.'

He glanced towards her, and so did Nick. She was some distance away, isolated, her young form erect and defiant but her hands fastened securely behind her. For a moment a heavy cloud drifted over the face of the moon, and she glanced up. It seemed the whole world was impenetrably gloomy for a while until the moonlight came back. The few glowing torches did little to alleviate the darkness.

'War gods angry!' the chief declared finally, swinging round, and though Nick and Hansford had difficulty in understanding his tongue, it presented no mystery to Betty. She waited in silence.

'You cheat war god!' the chief continued. 'Many men die because you cheat. So you suffer slow death as reward. Gods must be satisfied. Here! Too long to go back to settlement. Gods are angry. Must satisfy now. The white woman first. The white men shall watch. They must suffer the anguish of seeing death of white queen.'

'What's he saying, Bet?' Nick called to her. 'Things as tough as they look?'

'More than.' she answered, and she tried to keep the terror out of her voice. 'They're adding something to make dying as tough as it can be. Because we cheated them last time. And they're going to get busy right here — I'm to die first and you'll follow after watching me.'

Nick struggled savagely with his ropes. But there was just nothing he could do to budge them. Overhead, the moon vanished again behind a cloud-bank, and the torches gleamed all the more brightly in consequence. Betty made no moves to try and free herself;

she knew it would be useless. But she did keep looking at the sky.

Then as the moon reappeared she watched, instead, the activities of the Aztecs. Four of them were hauling a massive rough stone pillar, perhaps eight feet high, into position, supporting it upright by means of heavy stones around its somewhat sunken base. Presumably, it was to take the place of the fantastic wooden demon to which they usually prayed. Once the pillar was in place there began the operation of collecting brushwood from the surrounding valley side.

'Do you suppose they're going to burn her to death?' Nick panted, wet with perspiration.

'Why not?' Hansford's voice was toneless. 'They tried to do it before; I reckon they'll do it again, with interest.'

Nick looked about him desperately — towards the other members of the party lying bound not very far away. There was no possible chance of escape. The Redskins were everywhere, alert for every dubious move.

Then apparently the preparations were over. The moon vanished behind scudding cloud and a fresh wind sprang up over the basin. The torches were set down in a ring near the upright pillar so the scene of the sacrifice could be clearly viewed. Sickened, Nick and Hansford watched for what was to happen next.

So far, Betty had not been touched. She still stood in proud defiance, watching the sky. It even looked as though she might be praying. The wind was stirring her wealth of golden hair and setting her brief garments flapping.

Then began the dirge of the Redskins as, on their knees, they uttered incantations to the gods of their cult. This lasted perhaps five minutes under the clouded sky — then six of the braves, at a given order, marched forward to where Betty stood. For her to resist them was impossible. Holding her above their heads by shoulders and ankles they carried her to where the pillar stood; then they waded through the piled-up brushwood with her body resting on top of their heads.

Nick and Hansford strained to see what was happening but the intervening Indians blocked the view. Betty herself knew quite well what was intended, but no murmur of fear escaped her. She lay helpless on the heads of the Indians whilst one of the number shinned to the top of the pillar, fixed himself in position, then tossed down a rope. The braves below knotted it tightly through the cord already about Betty's ankles, then it was drawn up and fixed securely round the top of the pillar.

The braves supporting Betty began to back away until only one was remaining. He supported her head and shoulders for a moment and then began to lower her, until her back was hard against the stone. The rope took the strain of her weight and held firm. At an order from the chieftain she was raised again, her wrists freed from behind her — and then she dropped back helplessly to find her arms being drawn taut to either side of her and secured by a cord passing behind the pillar.

Nick gulped and swore blue murder as the Indians moved aside for a moment and he was able to see what had happened. Betty was fastened immovably to the pillar, head downwards, her arms spread crosswise to either side of her. Her rippling hair almost touched the piled-up brushwood.

'I can't stick this,' Nick panted hoarsely. 'Look what these filthy buzzards have done — '

'I'm looking,' Hansford answered bitterly, the scene all too clear in the moonlight. 'It isn't anything new to secure the victim upside down; they do it so the head of the victim isn't pointing the same way as that uv th' god — '

Wind whipped his face, bringing a stinging shower of dust. The Indians were dirging again, bowing low before

Betty's helpless figure. The only faint hope so far lay in the fact that the fire had not yet been lighted. Once that happened she would be dead within a few minutes, her hair would ignite first.

Nobody was more aware of the imminence of death than Betty herself — but she still had a last card to play. She knew from experience just how long the ceremony ought to take before the fire was lighted, and every second gained counted. Her worst difficulty lay in the fact that the Aztecs had suspended her by her feet. With her head downward it made it difficult for her to study the sky.

The sky! Everything depended on that. It was thickly clouded now and sand was blowing up into her face as she hung immovable. It seemed to her that the ceremony was taking an interminable time. She looked below her at the piled-up brushwood, then at the apparently inverted figures of the wailing braves — and, more distantly, the outline of her father and Nick, apparently hanging out of the ground.

It occurred to her, with sudden horror, that perhaps the ceremony was being unduly prolonged so as to inflict the maximum suffering upon her before death. If so, her last hope might never be realized. She might lose her senses before she could put her plan in action.

The wind came again, sighing and moaning this time through the stone buildings. Betty shut her eyes for a moment as blinding dust surged into them. Then she opened them again and forced her head up a little. She could dimly see her own suspended body and her feet held by the rope over the pillar top. Beyond was the sky, the clouds churning with moonlight behind them.

Betty relaxed again and prayed desperately for the one thing she needed. She was satisfied that the Aztecs were prolonging the ceremony so she could endure the full growing torture of her unnatural position before death relieved her.

'In heaven's name, Hansford, isn't

there something we can do?' Nick demanded. 'These filthy devils keep on chanting and bowing and get no nearer! Betty's been hanging there for nearly five minutes, I should think. She'll die anyway, without the fire, if she isn't cut down.'

'Yuh think I haven't thought of that?' Hansford whispered, his eyes fixed on her in the torchlight as she hung motionless. 'I'd sooner the skunks had done it ter me than her.'

'They'll do it to both of us afterwards — and to the boys over there,' Nick retorted. 'Betty's got it first for being the tribal leader. Why in hell can't they light the fire under her an' have done with it?'

He tore frantically at the thongs pinning his wrists, his huge chest muscles expanding to the limit under the effort — but the attempt was useless. By no possible feat of physical strength could he break free — and even if he did the braves were ready to attack. They stood nearby, knives in their hands, ready to make sure their sadistic sacrifice was not interrupted.

'I think the kid's dead or unconscious,' Nick said at last, breathing hard. 'Anyways, she isn't moving.'

Hansford said nothing. His eyes were blurred a little with tears. To have only just found his daughter and then lose her to so anguishing a death was almost more than he could stand.

But both he and Nick were wrong in assuming that Betty was dead — or unconscious. She was still very much alive, her lack of movement being caused only by the drag of the ropes. Her whole being was concentrated on the last throw she hoped to make — if it ever came.

It did come. She felt a spot of wet fall on her outstretched left arm. Then came more on her legs. With an effort she tried to get the inverted scene before her into focus.

'Hold!' she cried hoarsely, using the language of the Aztec tribe. 'Hold! I command you!'

The dirging abruptly stopped. The Indians looked at her fixedly in the torchlight. The elders moved forward, their feathers blowing in the wind.

'The white queen has last words?' the leader demanded.

'I give you warning,' Betty said breathlessly, and the strain of shouting made the blood-vessels pound behind her eyes. 'If you let me die the rain-gods will blight you forever! Already the rain-gods are angered. I command that they destroy you if you persist in the torture. Release me, that I may call off their wrath. Soon I die — and when I die, you die too.'

The Aztec Indians looked at one another sharply. Superstition, the one failing they had in common with all savages, was working upon them rapidly, the one fact on which Betty was relying. Even as she had finished speaking the drops of rain increased suddenly and the storm began to break in all its fury. Wind whirled across the basin, flinging dust and small stones before it.

'You lie!' the Aztec leader retorted. 'The rain-gods are not at your command!'

'I command them as you command the war-gods,' Betty answered, her words laboured. 'They are angered because you have hanged me thus, with my feet to the heavens and my head to the earth. It is an insult which will bring destruction on us all. Release me! Let me command the rain-gods to cease their fury — '

A whiplash of lightning and crack of thunder interrupted her. It came at the very second when it was needed. The Redskins looked up in alarm at the sky, the ground quaking under the impact of the thunder. They knew what the fury of the rain-gods meant — the destruction of their cattle, the flooding of their lands.

Betty could say no more. She was having difficulty in keeping her senses. Her legs had become numb and her head felt as if it would explode. The inverted scene before her was dancing crazily so she could no longer keep it in proper focus.

The Indians huddled amongst themselves, conversing. The rain came in a sudden deluge, reviving Betty somewhat with its coolness. She half closed her eyes to try to stop them aching so intolerably. For a long moment the Redskins contemplated her.

'Quick death appease war-god?' one of them suggested, and put the point of his knife against the girl's swollen jugular.

'No — rain-gods more powerful than war-gods,' the chief replied, thinking; then he started at another crack of thunder and deluge of rain.

'You die if I die.' Betty whispered, and the Redskins still hesitated, looking at her. She was about at the end of her endurance. Some ten minutes had passed since she had been hanged upside down, and the world was commencing to whirl around her.

'Release her!' the chief snapped suddenly. 'She must command the rain-gods to cease their fury!'

One of the braves stepped forward, huddled against the sweeping rain. He unfastened the rope which held Betty's hands behind the pillar and they dropped limply below her head. She still was conscious, but incapable of movement. Dimly she realized her bursting head was being raised, that sinewy hands were gripping beneath her armpits as her feet were slashed free — Then she collapsed suddenly into the brushwood and lay breathing hard, her legs dead from cramp.

Very slowly she began to get up, staggering as the world seemed to rock. Her arms were seized and she was half lifted over the brushwood and set down.

'Command the gods to cease their fury!' the chief ordered.

She gradually got a grip on herself, the dizziness passing. Looking up at the sky, she raised her hands over her head.

'Cease, I command you!' she cried.

'Think she'll make it?' Nick whispered tensely to Hansford.

'She's got to — or die.'

'You have lied!' the Indian chief snarled presently.

'I must have time!' Betty insisted, twirling round urgently. 'You shall see! I rule the rain-gods and they'll obey. They still do not understand that you have released me — !'

She raised her hands again to the sky, going down on her knees at the same time. How long she kept murmuring words neither her father nor Nick could estimate, but it did become evident to them after a while that the wind was slackening. Just as rapidly the thunder died away and stars began to peep from amidst the ragged clouds.

Then at last the moon came through, shining pallidly on the mud which had been dust. Betty got up slowly. mud clinging to her bare knees.

'It is done,' she said, her voice coldly proud. 'The rain-gods have obeyed. Know you, chieftain, that I alone rule the rain-gods as you rule the war-gods. Let I and my paleface friends go in peace — or the wrath of the gods will descend again.'

The power of superstition worked. The Aztec chief stood aside.

'Go!' he ordered. 'We not quarrel with rain-gods. Rain-gods too powerful.'

Betty turned away with dignity, though she wanted to run. She went to where her father and Nick stood and unfastened their ropes.

'Nice going,' Nick whispered. 'What the heck did you do, anyway?'

'Tell you later when we're clear of here. Let's free the other men before the chief changes his mind.'

Moving sedately, despite the desire to dash for it, the trio went over to where the other members of their party were bound and lying in the mud. It was only a matter of a few seconds to release them.

'We'll walk away,' Betty said, glancing back over her shoulder to where the impassive Indians stood watching. 'It won't look so much like an escape as it would on horses.'

'Lead on,' Nick murmured, and, holding Betty's arm, he stayed beside her as they went up the valley slope. When they had got as far as the woodland they began to breathe again. There were no signs of pursuit.

'I still don't get it.' Nick persisted.

'Being a tribal queen came in useful finally,' Betty responded, as they made their way along. 'Of all the tribes, the Aztecs are perhaps the most superstitious. They fear the wrath of the gods more than anything. Before they strung me up I noticed a storm was blowing up, and from past experience I knew it would last only a short period. The Aztecs, having moved up from south of the territory, are not yet acquainted with the climate. So I pinned my hopes on the storm starting — which it did — and the fact that it would soon stop, apparently after I commanded it to do so. That, with superstitious Indians, carried more weight than all the knives and guns in creation.'

'Good girl,' Nick murmured, hugging her to him. 'And what about your town? Do you still want to be 'Glorious Smile' or have you had enough?'

'After tonight's ordeal more than enough,' she replied quietly. 'In any case, with the Aztecs dominating the territory, all peace has gone. I'm going with you — and dad — to white man's territory.'

'And we've a tough job ahead of us,' Nick said seriously. 'To get to some-wheres safe, I mean. I guess we can drink at streams and eat berries, but we — '

'We'll make it,' Hansford said reso-lutely. 'I reckon we oughta after all we've dodged so fur. If we keep on goin' we can hit Tascosa in Texas. We'll be OK then.'

But it was easier said than done. With no horses to carry them and wild land to cover the journey was gruelling. Wherever possible they kept to the cover of the forests and by this means dodged whatever foes there might be and also found edible roots and berries to sustain them. Because she was a vigorous, open-air girl Betty survived the journey to Tascosa as much as the men with her.

They had no real idea how long it was before they at last sighted Tascosa in the shimmering distances. Footsore and weary, they emerged from the woodland to see the town some five miles distant.

'We made it,' Nick murmured, bearded and grimy. 'Taken us a few days too — And right here, Betty, seems as good a time as any for me to mention that I'm still holdin' out that offer for you to be Mrs. Carson. I can protect you best that way.'

Betty gripped his arm gently. He needed no other answer.

We do hope that you have enjoyed reading this large print book.

Did you know that all of our titles are available for purchase?

We publish a wide range of high quality large print books including:
Romances, Mysteries, Classics
General Fiction
Non Fiction and Westerns

Special interest titles available in large print are:
The Little Oxford Dictionary
Music Book, Song Book
Hymn Book, Service Book

Also available from us courtesy of Oxford University Press:
Young Readers' Dictionary
(large print edition)
Young Readers' Thesaurus
(large print edition)

For further information or a free brochure, please contact us at:
Ulverscroft Large Print Books Ltd.,
The Green, Bradgate Road, Anstey,
Leicester, LE7 7FU, England.
Tel: (00 44) **0116 236 4325**
Fax: (00 44) **0116 234 0205**

A TOWN CALLED TROUBLESOME

John Dyson

Matt Matthews had carved his ranch out of the wild Wyoming frontier. But he had his troubles. The big blow of '86 was catastrophic, with dead beeves littering the plains, and the oncoming winter presaged worse. On top of this, a gang of desperadoes had moved into the Snake River valley, killing, raping and rustling. All Matt can do is to take on the killers single-handed. But will he escape the hail of lead?

THE WIND WAGON

Troy Howard

Sheriff Al Corning was as tough as they came and with his four seasoned deputies he kept the peace in Laramie — at least until the squatters came. To fend off starvation, the settlers took some cattle off the cowmen, including Jonas Lefler. A hard, unforgiving man, Lefler retaliated with lynchings. Things got worse when one of the squatters revealed he was a former Texas lawman — and no mean shooter. Could Sheriff Corning prevent further bloodshed?

CABEL

Paul K. McAfee

Josh Cabel returned home from the Civil War to find his family all murdered by rioting members of Quantrill's band. The hunt for the killers led Josh to Colorado City where, after months of searching, he finally settled down to work on a ranch nearby. He saved the life of an Indian, who led him to a cache of weapons waiting for Sitting Bull's attack on the Whites. His involvement threw Cabel into grave danger. When the final confrontation came, who had the fastest — and deadlier — draw?

RIVERBOAT

Alan C. Porter

When Rufus Blake died he was found to be carrying a gold bar from a Confederate gold shipment that had disappeared twenty years before. This inspires Wes Hardiman and Ben Travis to swap horse and trail for a riverboat, the *River Queen*, on the Mississippi, in an effort to find the missing gold. Cord Duval is set on destroying the *River Queen* and he has the power and the gunmen to do it. Guns blaze as Hardiman and Travis attempt to unravel the mystery and stay alive.

McKINNEY'S LAW

Mike Stotter

McKinney didn't count on coming across a dead body in the middle of Texas. He was about to become involved in an ever-deepening mystery. The renegade Comanche warrior, Black Eagle, was on the loose, creating havoc; he didn't appear in McKinney's plans at all, not until the Comanche forced himself into his life. The US Army gave McKinney some relief to his problems, but it also added to them, and with two old friends McKinney set about bringing justice through his own law.

BLACK RIVER

Adam Wright

John Dyer has come to the insignificant little town of Black River to destroy the last living reminder of his dark past. He has come to kill. Jack Hart is determined to stop him. Only he knows the terrible truth that has driven Dyer here, and he knows that only he can beat Dyer in a gunfight. Ex-lawman Brad Harris is after Dyer too — to avenge his family. The stage is set for madness, death and vengeance.